A Medium's Christmas Gift

Becky Tibbs: A North Carolina
Medium's Mystery Series, Book 3

Chariss K. Walker

A Medium's Christmas Gift

I think fantasy thrillers excite audiences as, inherently, people have a fascination for the unknown and the unexplained.

– Krystle D'Souza

Chapter 1

Martin Jerome Smith was frustrated and feeling a little depressed. Normally, he was upbeat and outgoing. As a sergeant of Asheville's City Police Department, he didn't relish anyone knowing that he often had serious bouts of depression. He knew the cure for it; it only took one thing to turn his sadness into joy – and at the moment, he was jonesing for it.

Although it was true that he had a stressful job as a police officer, none of that seemed to bother Marty. He simply took his duties at work in stride.

Yep, Marty could bust a drug dealer and lock up a felon with ease. He could enter a dark house in a shady neighborhood after a blood-curdling 911 call without batting an eye. He could attend a traffic accident where the vehicle and its occupants were mangled and bloody without losing his lunch. Suffice it to say that it wasn't his job that bothered him.

The thing that got under his skin the most was that he couldn't seem to get the only girl he'd ever loved to commit to him. And, she was the drug he needed most right now. He was addicted to her.

Marty was frustrated because he'd had enough of her excuses. He felt certain that Barbara Tibbs cared about him as much as he cared for her, but she always had some justification, some idiotic and flimsy explanation for not moving forward in their relationship.

1

"My folks just died, let me adjust to that before we make our plans," she'd said.

"I want to finish my doctorate," she'd said.

"It's taking longer than I thought," she'd said.

Always some pigheaded excuse… Well, except for the one about her parents' death. That one was true and easily verified. Marty understood that she needed time to grieve and sort out things with her brother and sister.

Barb's parents had both died in a car accident nearly six years ago. In the antique business, Justin and Joyce Tibbs had made regular scouting trips to several nearby southern estate sales and auctions to pick up new-to-them merchandise for their successful store in the River Arts District. They'd been on their way home from Alabama when the accident happened.

Justin, Joyce, Barbara, Bobby, and Becky Tibbs.

That was the Tibbs family in a nutshell. They were close-knit, much closer than Marty had been to his parents. On that particular weekend, Barbara and Bobby had joined Becky at the family residence for the weekend and to await the return of their parents.

According to Barb, Justin and Joyce were always home by Sunday evenings in time for a family meeting and dinner. It was a tradition reserved for family only. It was also the reason he didn't get to see her on those nights. He'd often resented that he never got to say goodbye to Barb before she returned to Raleigh for the week.

At the time of the accident, Becky, the youngest, still lived at home with her parents. Bobby had his own place not far from the family home. And, Barbara – his Barbara, he often liked to say, was still a student at North Carolina State University where she lived just off campus in Raleigh.

Barb, Bobby, and Becky had all been together that night when the North Carolina State Police came to deliver the death notification. Barb still cried every time the subject came up. And, when she did, Marty felt helpless and more than a little useless.

Marty thought he'd given Barbara the time she needed and demanded, but then the excuses just kept coming. He now realized that after her parents died it was around the same time that their relationship had changed. He honestly felt that things just went downhill after that incident… and it bothered him a lot. He was almost certain that it caused his terrible mood swings.

He had a reason to be depressed; he wanted to start a family. He couldn't think of anyone else with whom he wanted to spend his life. He was elated whenever she was in Asheville and he could spend time with her, but lately, she seemed to put her family first and him last.

Marty had been in love with Barb for as long as he could remember. She was the drug he needed in order to maintain his sanity and he hated her excuses. Now, after recent events, he wondered what else could possibly get in their way. He wondered if she'd ever come home to him and to her Asheville family.

Presently, there was even more to bother him and he really didn't know how much more he could take. Barbara had been awfully skittish and elusive ever since Becky, her younger sister, was kidnapped and nearly died last month. That incident had become her latest excuse.

"Marty, our family just suffered a terrible trauma. Becky could've died. Give me some time to adjust to that," she'd said.

Chapter 2

Marty knew he hadn't done enough in the attempts to rescue Becky. Bobby had come to him with a tall tale he'd gotten from a ghost, but Marty was in a quandary. He couldn't simply trust or rely on the account of a ghost who had witnessed Becky's abduction. Why, he'd be laughed out of the police station.

No one else had seen a thing. No living person anyway. Marty had done the best he could, hadn't he? He'd assigned a new officer to look over the street cam footage. It was a weak effort to spot Becky's truck leaving the River Arts District.

But, his new officer, Detective Patrick Burns, was efficient and diligent. If it hadn't been for his insistence, they might not have found Becky in time. Marty felt guilty about that now, but at the time, he'd followed protocol.

"Does Barbara blame me for the near loss of her little sister?" he worried.

Marty had to admit that, in the beginning, he hadn't taken the threat of Becky's supposed kidnapping seriously. Everyone who was anyone knew that Becky Tibbs was a medium or psychic or something like that. He wasn't sure of the correct terminology for someone like Becky, but he was pretty sure she talked to dead people. Even though she was Barb's sister, Marty had to admit that Becky made him feel a bit uncomfortable.

"Oh, be honest about it!" He muttered. "She gives you the heebie-jeebies!"

He suspected that she made a lot of folks feel that way until they needed help with their own ghost problems. Then, they were over the top about Becky Tibbs. It was as if she'd suddenly hung the moon.

If he was going to be really honest, in truth, she'd helped him solve a murder with knowledge from the dead people with whom she talked. He wasn't comfortable with that knowledge even though his Captain had been happy to have a ten-year-old cold-case off the books.

As a detective, Marty had been trained to look for hard evidence. Everyone knew that the 'dead don't talk.' At least they didn't until Becky was around. Marty knew that good police work required that you let the evidence speak for itself.

He'd held fast to his training for his entire career, but that had all changed several months ago when Becky had asked Marty to look into the death of Josh Edwards, her boyfriend who had died on her birthday ten years ago.

He'd considered Josh's death an accident at best, an unsolved mystery at worst. However, hoping to score some points with Barbara, Marty had let Becky talk him into looking into the matter. Now, in hindsight, Marty could see that Becky had carefully and skillfully led him to the eventual conclusion – Josh was murdered.

"She manipulated me," he indignantly thought.

Marty had never been a believer in such paranormal stuff for sure and, even though he'd soon seen enough to realize that the girl had a gift, he was pretty certain that he couldn't trust it. He had plenty of questions about the things Becky Tibbs knew and could do.

If someone could see beyond the physical, if they could see things that no one else could see, well it just might indicate they were dangerous. Marty cringed at that thought.

As he continued his self-examination, he wondered more and more about Becky as he blamed her for Barbara's recent rebuffs. But, could he really go so far as to label Becky 'a danger to society?' If he did, he wondered how that would affect his relationship with Barbara.

He knew that's exactly what his Uncle Joe would say about Becky, but Marty wondered if he really believed the cute little girl he'd known for more than a decade, was something to fear. He'd gone to school with all the Tibbs kids –Barbara, Bobby, and Becky. True, Becky was four years younger and had been only a freshman when he and Barbara were seniors, but to label her as psychotic was over the top even for him, wasn't it?

Marty's Uncle Joe, a psychiatrist from Columbia, would say the young woman was delusional and a threat to society, but the old man worked with real wackadoos. He often talked about his patients' bizarre hallucinations and the medications he prescribed to keep their fallacies at bay. Did Becky need a really strong dose of Haldol?

Marty couldn't help but wonder what else the young Tibbs girl knew. He wondered if she knew anything about him. And, that very thought pressed his paranoia button.

He recalled how Becky had known Josh's father, Bradley Edwards, had killed his own son. She'd untangled connections and hidden motives that the police would've never solved without her help.

Marty shuddered again when he remembered the glass pendants and pipes magically flying around Bradley Edwards's distribution shop. Those objects appeared to have a life of their own. Then, all the glass artwork had violently slammed onto the glass-topped counters which had shattered from the forcefulness. Slivers and shards of glass had exploded, filling the air.

Marty's cheek had been cut as he watched the bizarre event in awe. All his instincts told him to run, but he hadn't run. He didn't know if he was frozen to the spot or simply curious, but he hadn't run.

When he told Bobby and Becky about what he'd seen, Becky had calmly said that Josh's ghost would continue to torment his father until he confessed.

And, Bradley Edwards did confess.

Sure, Marty had made the arrest but he knew the credit belonged to Becky. He'd had no problem admitting it to himself, but he rarely acknowledged it to anyone else.

Still, even after everything he'd witnessed during that case, he just couldn't shake his old beliefs and thought patterns about the entire situation. He'd always believed that when you died, you were just dead, but everything he'd learned while working that case had shaken his worldview.

The jolting gyrations he'd experienced were very similar to an earthquake. Life after death no longer seemed simple or cut and dried to him. But, the earth had settled again after the quaking was done and Marty had returned to his former beliefs.

Chapter 3

Marty Smith continued to assess the situation that surrounded the Tibbs family. It was truly a sad tragedy the night their parents died and he assumed he knew everything there was to know about each one of the survivors. He felt connected to them through Barbara and Marty supposed he understood that it had changed their lives. He pretended to accept that their misfortune had also rolled over his life and flattened it as well.

What Marty Smith didn't know about the night Barb's parents died could've filled a book and, if he had known, it certainly would've shaken his fairytale world to bare rubble this time.

He had no idea that Justin and Joyce made it home to their children the night they'd died at the I-40 and I-240 bottleneck wearing their new and improved ghostly forms.

He had no inkling that just before the police officer knocked on the door of the Tibbs residence, Justin and Joyce had wandered back home in confusion about how they got there.

He had no awareness whatsoever that even though the state trooper couldn't see Mr. and Mrs. Tibbs, that Barb, Bobby, and Becky had clearly seen their now dead parents.

He didn't know that Justin had stood toe-to-toe with the officer arguing that he was very much alive. At least, Justin had argued his case until he'd finally accepted his fate.

And he most certainly did not understand that the gift of sight, a gift bestowed on Barbara, Bobby, and Becky was an inherited gift, a nonrefundable gift that didn't allow for returns or exchanges.

There was a lot Marty Smith didn't know about that night, but it couldn't all be blamed on Barbara. He was also responsible for the secrets that could eventually tear them apart because he honestly didn't want to know.

Since Marty had been credited with finding Becky Tibbs, his captain had rewarded him. This was his first unscheduled day off in a while. He was so gung-ho about his job that he really didn't know what to do with the extra time. He drove around the city as his mind roamed freely through the years he'd spent loving Barbara Tibbs.

Suddenly, an unbidden and startling thought occurred to him. *"Do I really want to marry into the Tibbs family where such paranormal actions are accepted and considered normal?"*

Bobby and Barbara acted as if everything Becky did was routine. They accepted her weird ability as normal and even plausible. Would that cause problems for him and Barbara if they were to marry? Would he have to fake his acceptance of her younger sister? Feeling the way he did about Becky, could he do that?

Marty knew he wasn't very good at hiding his true feelings about anything. As he pushed those thoughts to the back-burner of his mind, his thoughts meandered back to Barbara… He'd spent the better part of his life with her.

Barbara had been his only romantic interest. Sure, he'd flirted with other girls and a pretty woman caught his eye on occasion, but Barbara had his heart.

They'd dated in high school and throughout college in spite of the distance. Barb was damned and determined to get her education at UNC in Raleigh while he'd had to remain at UNC in Asheville.

It wasn't his choice and they hadn't planned it that way. It was simply the way things had worked out. Even though they'd always intended to go to Raleigh together, Marty's father had gotten sick, very sick, just before their graduation. Marty had felt obligated to stay close to home in case he was needed. Sometimes, his father's disease was worse than at other times, and Marty was needed often.

Still, Marty and Barbara had managed to see each other and be together whenever they could, and, as far as he knew, neither one of them had dated anyone else. He knew he certainly hadn't... He'd only had eyes for Barbara.

He'd always wanted to marry her.

As he considered this new feeling about Becky and whether or not he could fake his acceptance of her, Marty had to admit that he didn't know a lot about the Tibbs family history. He knew they'd moved to Asheville in the early 1940s from Georgia and had always been in the antique's business. In fact, the store that Becky now owned in the River Arts District was originally owned by her grandparents, passed to her father, Justin Tibbs, who then passed it on to his three children.

That was another curious situation – Barbara and Bobby had quickly signed over their interests in the store and the family home to Becky. Barbara had said, "It's only right that Becky own both, after all, she'll run the shop and use the money earned for the upkeep of the home."

Somehow, that didn't sit right with Marty either.

Chapter 4

As far as he knew, the Tibbs family didn't have any psychopaths or murderers dangling from their ancestral tree. Unfortunately, Marty couldn't say the same for his own history. His family was one of the oldest in Asheville. The Smiths had been around for generations and could trace their lineage directly to Daniel Smith, commonly called 'Daniel Boone of Buncombe County.'

It was well-known that Daniel Boone had fought the Cherokees in the area. His commitment had very nearly wiped out their entire tribe. Marty had always thought it was a bloody, disgusting legacy and admittedly he often felt ashamed of his heritage. He'd felt his ancestors were outwardly god-fearing, but heathens underneath where it counted, especially when compared to the Tibbs family.

His mind wandered quite a bit as he tried to sort out the reasons for his discontent. Finally, it traveled back to the idea that Barbara wasn't being honest or open with him lately – that she seemed distant. He considered her actions to be secretive and it really bothered him that she might be hiding something.

He was out of sorts and angrily grumbled as he looked around his personal car. He spotted his packed go-bag on the floorboard and made a hasty decision.

"Damned if I'm going to have any more of it!" He angrily thought. *"It's time for her to make a decision and quit stringing me along. I need to know. I have a right to*

know. She either loves me or she doesn't. Even if I have to force her hand, I want an answer. We're not getting any younger. We should be buying a house together and starting our own family. If we were doing that, maybe she wouldn't be consumed and attached to her birth family.

These feelings had culminated when he witnessed young Patrick Burns fall for Becky Tibbs. From the many dreamy-eyed looks on Patrick's face, the young man had fallen hard. Becky had readily accepted Patrick's interest and they were now dating. Even more surprising, Patrick didn't even mind that Becky talked to dead folks.

Marty thought about Becky's strange ability again, but it wasn't only Becky that was odd. There had always been something unusual about the Tibbs family, something he couldn't put his finger on. He'd felt it every time he was around any one of them, and, even though he didn't want to admit it, he finally understood that the peculiar aspects also included Bobby and Barbara.

Even as teenagers the Tibbs kids had an uncanny ability to discern, suss-out things, and know what to do in almost any situation. It was an unexpected characteristic that he'd admired in his teen years. It was only one of the many reasons he'd loved and respected Barbara. It was one of the reasons he was still friends with Bobby. Marty wondered if that bizarre sensitivity was a precursor to the gift that Becky had.

It was apparent that Barbara and Bobby accepted their little sister's gift, almost as if it was an extension of their own. They trusted it, liked it, and defended it.

And, that's when the reality of all his troubles finally occurred to Marty Smith– "Damn!" He exclaimed, "They're also psychics or mediums or whatever one wants to call it!"

He realized that it was the answer to all the previous questions that had eluded him. Bobby and Barbara had the same ability to see ghosts as Becky did. That's how Bobby was able to report what a ghost had witnessed the day his sister was abducted. The ghost told Bobby!

"Does it run in families?" he wondered. If he and Barbara married, would they end up with a little psychic baby he'd despise?

He was flabbergasted.

How could he have missed that?

Already traveling on I-240 East, he suddenly merged onto I-40 East and settled in for the three-and-a-half-hour drive to Barbara's apartment in Raleigh.

"Yup, I'm going to get some damn answers today," he solemnly vowed.

Chapter 5

"Becky?" Joyce called out. "Becky, can I stop in to see you? Please, honey, I'm really sorry about interfering with your Thanksgiving meal."

Becky ignored her mother and didn't reply.

"Please, honey, I know you're mad at me, but don't hate me." The disembodied speech filled the kitchen while Becky sat at the island breakfast bar. She drank her first cup of morning coffee and continued to work a Sudoku puzzle, effectively ignoring her mother.

"How long are you going to punish me, honey?" Joyce implored. "I feel terrible enough, especially after your abduction. We could've lost you for good... well; Bobby and Barbara would've lost you. Your father and I would've gained you on this side, but that can't happen yet. It's not the time for that. You haven't even really lived yet. Besides, you're needed on that side. You still have a lot of work to do. It's a very good thing that nice young detective didn't give up until he found you, huh? Come on, honey, talk to your dear, old mother."

Joyce's mention of Patrick brought him to the front of Becky's thoughts. It was odd. Ever since she'd met him, she'd felt more confident, more at home in her own skin, and more at ease with her chosen path in life. She'd felt truly accepted and important to him. His approval had influenced the way she now viewed herself.

Funny how that can change a girl's life, she silently mused, determined to keep her mother locked out of her life and thoughts. One thing she knew for sure, ghosts couldn't read your mind.

Now, it was different for spiritual companions or spirit guides, what some people called guardian angels. They *could* read your mind and you could read theirs if attuned to it. In fact, a person could hear their spiritual companions all the time because their spirit guides had been with them since birth.

Zetmeh had explained:

> *You've heard me so often, my dear one, that you think it is your own thoughts and wise counsel that you follow.*

Joyce kept pleading her case and Becky tuned her mother's ghost out. Thoughts of Patrick filled her mind and heart. They hadn't seen each other since Friday night when she'd cooked dinner for him, but the tingling sensation, the electric charge she'd felt when they'd touched that first time rushed back to her. It washed over her entire being and brought joy to her lower chakras.

Zetmeh, always a wealth of information, had also explained about the seven major chakras, and as she'd shared those details, Becky had felt each one tingle and glow as if ignited:

> *You have seven major chakras, dear one. There are three lower chakras, a bridge, and three higher chakras. We will begin at the lowest and work our way to the highest, my child.*

*The root chakra concerns itself with family
and community. It influences our acceptance of self
and our beginnings. If that family and community
are loving and nurturing, the root chakra is healthy.
It is located at the lowest part of the torso, between
our legs. Think of it as the roots of a tree as it digs
deeply into the life we've been given. Its color is red
like red earth or rubies.*

*The sacral chakra concerns itself with
pleasures, those very things that make us happy. If
we are taught to feel shame at an early age, the
sacral chakra is unhealthy. Think of it as a beacon,
a light that attracts those things that we desire to
experience in order to understand what we like and
what we don't like. It influences our joy and is
located between the pubic area and navel. Its color
is orange.*

*The solar plexus chakra concerns itself with
our ego or self-image. If we experience approval at
a very early age, that chakra is healthy. Think of
this chakra as an indicator of the many experiences
we have tried; it's a gut-check. We either accept or
reject those occurrences as our self-image. It
influences our acceptance of who we are, where we
began, and what we like. It's located in the solar
plexus area or above the navel and below the breast
bone. Its color is yellow.*

*The heart chakra concerns itself with love,
love of self, love of family, and love of community. If
we know love as a young child, that chakra is
healthy. Think of the heart chakra as a bridge
between the physical plane, those three lower
chakras, and the spiritual plane, the three upper
chakras. It allows all that we know about ourselves
to move into love for even more personal and*

spiritual growth. It's located in the heart area of the body and its color is green.

The throat chakra concerns itself with our personal truth. If we were allowed to openly communicate without being shushed and made to feel insignificant as a child, the chakra is healthy. It influences our ability to speak and communicate our truthful purpose to others. Think of it as a megaphone. It broadcasts our truth, but it can blow people away if not tempered with love. It's located in the hollow of the throat or Adam's apple and its color is sky blue or aquamarine.

The third-eye chakra concerns itself with our vision of the world, the way we see life around us, and our future. If our insight was appreciated as a child, this chakra is healthy. Think of it as binoculars or a spyglass that gives us a more complete picture. It magnifies our ability to see, such as your gift as a medium. It's located in the brow or forehead, slightly above and between our two natural eyes. Its color is dark blue or lapis lazuli.

The crown chakra is located on the crown of the head. It represents our connection to the Divine mind. Not many of our childhood experiences can block our link to the spiritual plane, but the context can become distorted from the abuse suffered as a child. The crown chakra concerns itself with our spiritual and personal growth during each lifetime. Think of it as a gateway, a union with and to the ethers. Its color is crystal or the lightest shade of amethyst.

This young man, Patrick, ignites your three lower chakras and brings love to your heart chakra. As I've just said, the heart is the bridge between the earthly plane and the spiritual plane. Your love for him will bring much joy and personal and spiritual growth to your life, my dear one. We are happy for you.

Now, all Becky had to do was 'think' about Patrick and the powerful, lovely feeling returned. She wondered if it was the same for him. She blushed lightly as she hoped that is was. However, since it was already Wednesday and they were having coffee this morning, she supposed that she'd find out soon enough.

"I don't hate you, Mother," Becky finally said as she gathered up her keys and coat. "I just don't want to talk to you right now. I have to get to work."

Chapter 6

When Becky arrived at the antique shop she owned in the River Arts District, Jacob, Lois, and Myrtle were already there waiting for her arrival, but they were not alone. A new ghost, a young man in his early twenties, was standing with them.

Jacob, always the helper ghost, made it a priority to help any new ghost who didn't immediately cross over. If he couldn't solve their problems he felt bound to bring the newly departed spirit to Becky. Lois and Myrtle, always curious about everything, were Jacob's sidekicks.

Becky took her time as her eyes traveled over the newly dead. She realized this young ghost had to be left over from the fire. She wondered why they hadn't helped him Friday evening when the disaster had happened.

"Where has he been and why has he just now surfaced?" She silently asked herself.

He was covered in a thick layer of black soot and he'd been injured… From the looks of things and the way he held his hands over his abdomen, he'd been shot. Becky surmised that he'd most likely died before the fire broke out, but she couldn't be sure about that.

"I take it that this is mostly unrelated to the fire?" Becky asked Jacob. He nodded. "What is your name and how can I help you?" Becky inquired as she turned her gaze back to the young ghost.

"I'm Hank and I guess I was in the wrong place at the wrong time."

"What do you mean?" Becky asked, feeling as if his answer was too flippant, too rehearsed.

"I live, ahem, lived in Pueblo, Colorado. I came to Asheville to get away from the crack and heroin dealers in Colorado, but I still wanted to smoke a little weed."

"So you thought that even though weed is illegal in Asheville, it was a place where you could live and smoke weed when you wanted it?" Becky, not really sure where this was going, noncommittally recapped his admission.

"Well yeah. It's not legal but it's harmless, and here, if you get caught with less than an ounce the penalty isn't severe. Besides, there's a lot of research that shows it is beneficial to users, especially users with PTSD and emotional trauma."

"Do you have PTSD or some kind of emotional trauma?"

"I didn't want to get into my personal history or life," Hank explained. "But, if you insist, then I admit that we had a medical card in Pueblo and I believe that it will soon be legal in all states for medical use. I mean, it should be. It's far better than the harsh, chemical drugs that are currently used to treat the emotionally traumatized."

"We?" Becky asked.

Hank ignored her and continued, "Weed doesn't have the terrible side-effects that those chemical bombs have. Listen, I'm not here to argue or defend my use of marijuana."

"Then why are you here, Hank? How can I help you?" She kept her voice soft and controlled.

"I need your help with something else. Besides, you probably don't know this but heroin is cheaper than weed in some parts of the country. It's an epidemic. You know, now that weed is legal in a lot of states, the dealers have to compete in any way they can… so they lowered the price on hard drugs."

"He must really like pot to put up such a defense," Becky silently considered. Although she'd always felt that it was harmless, she held no strong personal convictions or judgments about its use – even though that wasn't always a popular or accepted opinion.

"So, what happened? How did you get shot? Did it have anything to do with drugs?" Becky asked, trying to keep Hank on track.

"Like I said, I guess I was in the wrong place at the wrong time," Hank replied. "I really don't remember much about it."

"Do you want to tell me who shot you? Do you want justice?"

"No, I need you to get this to my sister in Pueblo," Hank said as he dug into his jeans pocket and fished out a key. "She needs to get out of there now, sooner than we'd planned."

"Is she in danger?" Becky asked, beginning to see that the 'we' Hank had mentioned before pertained to his sister.

Yes, she's in serious danger. I came here to get a place for us to live together. She's nineteen. I found a place for us and the rent is paid for three months. That'll give her time to find a job and get her life together. I'm sorry to ask so much of you, but this is important to me. You see, our stepdad is mixed up with the cartel. My sister, Louise – I call her Lou-Lou – needs to get away from him. He's not a very nice man and he could do any dirty deed he wanted to do to Lou-Lou now that I'm not there to protect her. Our mother is totally out of her mind on crack… all the time. She quit watching out for us a few years back. Me and Lou-Lou were on our own. We made this plan to move here to Asheville and then I got myself killed, but that's no reason for her to stay there, especially when I've already got us a place set up... got her a place," Hank corrected.

Becky studied Hank for some moments. He wasn't highly educated, but he was smart, street-smart. She had no reason to disbelieve his story. From the description of his mother and stepdad, it sounded conceivable that he'd had a hard life. She was curious about his death, but she fully intended to help him even if he didn't want to share the details of his murder.

"Give me the information I need," she finally said.

Hank gave her Lou-Lou's phone number and Becky agreed to call her right then. Hank listened as Becky told Louise the sad story of her brother's death and his desire for her to leave Pueblo that very day.

As she talked to his sister, Hank's appearance changed. The black soot was gone and he no longer held onto his side where he'd been shot.

This was a common occurrence with ghosts. Once their unfinished business was resolved, they returned to their previous state in life. Becky noticed that beneath the black ash, Hank was a cute kid. Still, Becky wondered if the safety of his sister was Hank's only unfinished business. Wasn't he angry that his life had ended before he could enjoy a new, safe life in Asheville with Lou-Lou?

"Don't borrow trouble," Becky admonished herself. *"Just be happy for the win."*

Hank continued to listen to Becky's end of the conversation as the medium talked to Lou-Lou, "I'll keep the key here at my store. When you get to Asheville, call me. I'll pick you up at the bus station and take you to your new home. Can you manage that, Lou-Lou?"

"I can," the young woman tearfully agreed. "Do you know what happened to Hank's car? I'll need it once I get there."

"I'll try to find that out," Becky replied.

"I'll send a text when I have a bus schedule. That'll give you an idea of when I'll get there. Thank you, Becky. I hope to see you very soon... and thank you for helping my brother."

Becky didn't feel as if she'd actually helped Hank in the best way possible. Sure, she'd helped his sister start on her path to leave Pueblo, but she knew ghosts well. She was pretty certain that once Louise was safe, Hank would return with details of his murder. Ghosts liked to solve one problem at a time. Becky would be alarmed if he didn't want his murder solved because everyone, especially ghosts, needed closure.

Chapter 7

Patrick Burns parked his police car facing the street rather than in front of Becky's shop. He knew that most people would avoid a store if they thought the police were there. It was simply human nature. He didn't want his visits with Becky to drive her customers away.

He'd arrived promptly at eleven that morning to walk with Becky to the coffee shop where they would each drink a second cup of java and spend thirty minutes getting to know each other better. He wished it was longer, that he could spend more time with her, but they each had pressing responsibilities and little time for personal pleasures.

Besides, it wasn't as if he didn't already feel as if he knew her inside and out – he did. Patrick felt as if he'd known Becky his entire life. He just hadn't met her yet. Not until she was kidnapped anyway.

Once again he saw her pale, terrified face as she sat between the two very large women who had snatched her right out of this parking lot. One more time, he recalled Becky's near-to-death state as she lay helpless on the sofa in that remote farmhouse out in Hot Springs. She was lucky to be alive and he was even more fortunate that she liked him.

Becky watched Patrick through the store window with an admiring gaze. He was almost as tall as Bobby, and although not as broad, he was certainly fit and strong. With dark brown hair and hazel eyes, he was terribly cute, just the way she liked any romantic interest in her life.

She'd never liked 'pretty-boys' which was what she called any man who primped and preened, caring more about his looks than he did for her. She'd dated a few of that kind while in college, but it had never gone past the first kiss.

Becky shivered slightly when she thought about those kisses. It was like kissing a lizard, all tongue and hard, dry lips.

"Disgusting!" she muttered to no one in particular before she eagerly placed a "Be Back in Thirty" sign on the door and locked it. She was impatient to see Patrick again.

Jacob, Myrtle, and Lois had overheard Becky's mumbled outburst and stifled a chuckle behind their hands. Then, they each watched with delight as their favorite medium went outside to meet her new beau, an old-timey term they used when they referred to Patrick.

"Becky's new beau," the three ghosts giggled after she was out of earshot.

When Patrick took her arm to walk by her side, once more, they both felt the electric sensation that had passed between them on Friday evening. Becky jumped back a little. It wasn't that she didn't enjoy the mysterious feeling; she was just surprised at its intensity.

"I'm sorry," she quickly apologized. "The feeling just surprised me… it's so strong."

"I really like it," Patrick admitted. His hazel eyes twinkled as he grinned at her. "It makes me feel special that you feel it too."

"Have you felt that with anyone else?"

"Are you kidding?" he asked in surprise, but when he saw that she was serious, he said, "No, I've never felt anything like that before. At best, I've felt butterflies. At worst, I've felt revulsion. This, this sensation I feel with you and about you, is definitely a first. It's unique. It's magic."

Becky blushed at his words and thought to herself, *"He's not only cute, but he's also just plain sweet. Someone reared their son the right way."*

They continued to the coffee shop in silence. After he led Becky to a booth, he went to get their coffees in real mugs, just like they both liked.

Once he was seated across from her, Becky asked, "Do you feel that when we are apart? I mean, do you feel it when you think about me?"

"I was going to ask you the same thing," he smiled again, "but yes, all I have to do is think about you and I feel it just like I do when we touch. It's kind of amazing when you consider it."

"Do you suppose it will wear off?"

"I hope not!" Patrick confessed.

"Me too," Becky admitted.

The coffee break ended too soon and as he walked her back to the antique shop, they were silent. Just as they were outside her door, he asked, "Any more unusual ghost business today?"

"Well yes, funny that you should ask."

"Let me guess," Patrick interjected, "A gunshot victim?"

"How did you know?"

"The firemen found a body while clearing away the debris yesterday. He wasn't a resident of the apartments and they aren't sure how he ended up there. Did he happen to tell you who shot him?"

"No, he says he doesn't remember, but I suspect he doesn't want to recall it just yet. He only wanted me to get a message to his sister in Pueblo. Does it make you feel weird to talk to me about ghosts?"

"Are you kidding?" He asked. Becky realized it was his favorite phrase and she stifled a chuckle with a cough.

"I mean," Patrick continued, "I don't like that it puts you in harm's way, but I find it fascinating that you help them find peace and resolution."

"You're the first person who has ever said that to me, Patrick. I guess, you've been thinking about this a lot," Becky concluded.

"Indeed," Patrick said with another dimpled smile. "The way I figure it, if I want you in my life, and I do want you in my life, Becky Tibbs, then I have to accept any and everything about you. Your brother told me that very thing when we were at the fire Friday night. I guess I've been considering what that meant ever since. I can easily accept this as long as it allows me to be with you. I'm really glad we don't have any secrets between us."

"A little mystery is good, but I agree that secrets aren't good for anyone who wants to be close. I suppose Bobby is right. It's part of who I am. I can't change it and I'm very glad that you don't want me to."

"I really don't want you to change it," he assured.

"Patrick, did you believe in ghosts before you met me?"

She had to know if his acceptance of her ability was truly genuine. Did he already believe that what she did was possible or did he only believe in it because she said it was so? It was important to her to find out now before things went any further.

"Let's just say that I hoped it was true," Patrick slowly replied as he carefully chose his words. "I hoped that I wasn't crazy because you see, sometimes I smell my grandfather's cologne, Old Spice. Well, I actually smell it a lot of the time. I should say that I smell it when I'm on the job and possibly in danger. It's during those times that I feel like he is with me, watching over me."

As Patrick prudently chose his words to explain, an elderly gentleman suddenly appeared by his side. He wore wire-rimmed glasses. His hair was long, almost shoulder-length, and gray. He wore a brown suede jacket and a matching wide-brimmed hat. He patted Patrick lightly on the shoulder and gazed at Becky with clear, green eyes that twinkled like his grandson's when he smiled.

"He is here," Becky acknowledged and then went on to describe the elderly gentleman.

"That's my Grandpa Gus," Patrick proudly replied as his voice filled with awe. "Mr. Augustus Patrick Burns. Dang it! I knew it. I really knew it. He watches over me."

Becky listened to Gus and then repeated, "Your grandfather just wants you to know that you are never alone or forgotten. That he loves you very much and he's proud of you."

Patrick was overcome with a flood of gratitude as he considered his grandfather's words. When he spoke again, his words sent shivers of joy through Becky, "So you see, Becky, I was already a believer. You only made it real and tangible. Thank you and thank you, Grandpa Gus."

Becky smiled, "I'm glad."

"Dinner Friday night at your place?" Patrick asked as he quickly recovered from the emotional meeting.

"Yes," she agreed.

"Can I come over early and help?"

"Absolutely."

Patrick gently squeezed her hand and they both smiled as the tingling charge ran through their bodies. He was glad that Becky didn't jump away this time. He turned to leave, but before he'd taken two steps he turned back and leaned in to kiss her gently on the lips. "Thank you," he softly whispered.

Although the sensation caused her to feel breathless, and even a little dizzy, Becky's mind perceived several key and critical details: his lips were soft and supple, not dry and thin; he didn't try to shove his tongue down her throat which was something she really appreciated for a first kiss;

and last, but not least, his kiss had started a fire burning in the center of her being.

When she looked into his eyes, she saw embers of that same fire burning in Patrick's soul. Then, he was gone, leaving her to eagerly anticipate their next date on Friday evening.

Becky sighed deeply and then returned to the store. As she opened the door, she received a text message from Lou-Lou that said, "The bus leaves around three-thirty this afternoon. It arrives in forty-eight hours."

Becky gave the news to Jacob and Hank and then carried on with her day

.

Chapter 8

Meanwhile, Marty Smith had arrived in Raleigh at Barbara's apartment. She wasn't home, but determined to get some answers; he decided to wait for her. When she hadn't returned in an hour, however, he grew impatient and called her.

"Hi Marty," she answered.

Although he was glad that she took his call, it threw him off-guard a bit. He'd been prepared to leave a message because lately, more often than not, she hadn't answered his calls. He stumbled over the words he wanted to say and the uncertainty caused him to feel foolish, "Barb… uh, I'm in Raleigh at your apartment. Uh, I want to talk. Uh, when will you be home?"

"You're there now?" she faltered.

"I'm parked outside your apartment building right now," he repeated, "and, as I said, we need to talk."

It seemed that those words never boded well for any couple regardless of who said them. They always instigated several erratic thoughts in the one hearing them – what's wrong, what did I do now, oh crap, and so on.

"Well, I have class in an hour and then I have a doctor's appointment," Barb hedged. "It could be a couple of hours before I'm home."

"A doctor's appointment? Is something wrong? Are you ill?"

"No, it's just a monthly check-up," she lied. She'd never told Marty that she saw a therapist every month to keep her psychic abilities from ruining her life. She sure didn't want to tell him now.

Barbara suspected that if Marty knew about her gift that it would be the last she saw of him. In one small way that would be an answer to her prayers. She hated the lying and the deception, but it was even more difficult to think of life without Marty in it even though she had kept her relationship with him private even from Bobby and Becky. She'd loved him for as long as she could remember, but she was also certain that he would leave her if he knew her secret. She took a moment to question her certainty of that truth.

"Am I being selfish?" She silently wondered. "Am I holding onto something with him that I should've released years ago? If I had told Marty the truth after my parents died and if I had admitted then that I could see ghosts, would we be at this point right now? Would he have moved on and found someone else to love? Would this 'thing' between us… would it have become a thing of the past?"

Barb felt confused and she blamed the Xanax for that. It clouded her thinking processes and made it more difficult for her to reason things out like a normal person. It was all she could do to stay focused in class, so she'd put her studies first and allowed everything else to simply wait.

"Well, you said you have an hour before your next class. Can we talk now?"

Fearing the worst, Barb asked, "I don't know, Marty… what's this about?"

Tired of the delay, Marty blurted, "I want to know if you see ghosts the way your little sister does. I have to know the truth even if I can't accept it. Even if you've been lying to me all these years. I have to know if that's the real reason behind all the excuses you make… Why you won't commit to me and agree to marry me and move home. You won't even give me a date as to when you'll complete your coursework. It seems like you use your doctorate as an excuse to put me off every time I try to get a decision from you. I've had it, Barbara. I need some answers!"

Barbara was stunned and silent, too silent. The quiet grew deafening and spoke volumes to Marty. He knew that he'd finally hit the nail on the head. She didn't even bother to deny anything, but even if she had, he wasn't sure he'd believe her now.

"You're not denying it so I guess it's true," Marty quietly acknowledged. "Why didn't you tell me? Why did you lead me on like this?"

Barb was confused. It sounded as if he admitted that their relationship was over. If she was like Becky and saw ghosts, then everything was over between them. Was that what Marty meant?

Damn Xanax! She mentally ranted. *I can't make heads or tails out of this. Is this an ultimatum? Is Marty breaking up with me? Will I be devastated or relieved if it's true?*

"You know, they say that silence is consent. Is that what your silence means, Barb. Are you agreeing with the things I've just said?" Marty demanded.

"Do you still want to talk to me in person?" Barb whispered.

"Yeah, I'd prefer it!" Marty stormed.

"I'll be there in fifteen minutes."

Chapter 9

By the time, Barbara arrived, Marty had changed. He'd transformed into the spurned lover, the cuckold, the pathetic bastard who'd been deceived by the one he loved for more years than he cared to count.

He was bitter, but he still wanted answers.

Barbara put on a bright face, a smile that she didn't feel, unlocked her apartment door, and waved to Marty. He was still sitting in his car, but he slowly got out and came toward her. He stood there looking at Barb for a few, long moments, his face blank and unseeing.

"Come in," she encouraged and, once inside, they sat on her pale beige sofa a yard apart. It was the same sofa where they had made love. It was where they had cuddled to watch a movie. It was the sofa where he'd told her about his father's illness, the cases he'd worked, his promotion, and various other topics that affected his life.

Barb realized that Marty had shared much of his life on this sofa but she hadn't done the same. As the memories flitted through her mind, she also realized that she'd always felt stiff and withholding. She'd never actually bared her soul with Marty or been truly intimate with him. She'd been afraid to do so.

"Can I get you something to drink?" she offered, trying to smile, trying to be hospitable. As her lips turned up, her cheeks quivered in uncertainty.

"No, just tell me everything. Start at the beginning and don't leave anything out," he ordered.

His gruff voice surprised her. He'd never talked to her that way, but she could only imagine that it was the tone he used to interrogate suspects. She shuddered as she wondered if anything she had to say would matter now. Would it make any difference? She felt certain she had waited too long and, regardless of what she told him, Marty had already decided their future – a future that no longer included her.

Feeling anguish and hoping he would see reason, Barbara started at the beginning; she started with the night her parents had died six years ago. It was the night that she, Bobby, and Becky had seen their parents' ghosts just before the North Carolina State Trooper had arrived to give the death notification.

She gave Marty the cliff notes, but she didn't leave out any details. She admitted that she didn't want any part of it and that she took medication to block her ability. She told him all of it, everything that had happened since that unusual and fateful night.

He didn't ask any questions, he didn't interrogate her as she had feared. He simply listened, but the more she talked, the more she admitted the truth, Barb noticed that, if it was possible, Marty's features grew even harder. His jaw set in anger and the vein on the side of his neck throbbed with each beat of his heart.

He was unmoving.

After she'd finished the confession, he didn't have to tell her that their love affair was over; she could see it on his face. Her self-examination and questions about whether it would have been better to let him go years ago were now forgotten. Knowing that he no longer wanted her, made her want to hold on tighter.

If the Xanax hadn't kept her so off-balance and cloudy, Barb might've seen this outcome as a good thing just like she had earlier. Now, it simply hurt. It was as if a knife cut into her heart.

Still, she wanted to know why he couldn't accept the truth about her. She wanted to hear him say it. Why did it make any difference to him that she was a medium? Why did he care? It had nothing to do with him. She couldn't change who she was even though she desperately wanted to change that about herself. God only knew how she'd tried every drug out there with little success in an effort to stop her ability.

Still, she didn't understand why the truth had so drastically changed his affections for her. Now, she needed to know as urgently as Marty had needed to know the truth earlier. When she finally gathered the courage to ask, she regretted it immediately.

His reply was caustic, "Don't you understand? Can't you get it through your thick head?" Marty asked, using words he'd have never used with her before this moment. "I'm an officer of the law; I'm sworn to uphold the law, to serve and protect the people. I can't possibly love or marry someone who goes against everything I believe, who challenges my core beliefs about life and death. They say the truth sets you free and I finally understand – now, I'm free from this delusion.

"The truth? You want the truth? Brace yourself dear because you won't like it. The honest truth is that I can't associate with someone that every medical professional in the world considers dangerous. Most psychiatrists would judge you and your family as an extreme threat to normal people. Some would even have you committed, locked away, which is probably where you belong. And, although the jury was still out until today, I now agree with them. I'm sorry, Barbara, but whatever we had is over."

Marty stood up and then briskly walked to the door without looking back. It was as if he couldn't get away from her fast enough. He let himself out and was gone. He hurried to his car while Barbara was still frozen on the sofa.

"How could someone who has always been so gentle and respectful to me in the past become so hostile and hateful now?" she muttered in disbelief.

She heard her mother whisper, "No, darling, he was always that way. He simply hid it from you as you hid your gift from him. Your father and I have watched Marty Smith for some time now and this was always the only possible outcome. He was never going to accept you once he knew you were a medium."

"If you knew everything about him, you wouldn't want him either. Please don't beat yourself up about it. Just let it go and realize that you are now better off," her father advised.

"There is someone else out there for you. Someone much better than Marty Smith who will love you for who you are and accept everything you are," Joyce encouraged.

Barbara reached for the bottle of Xanax and took several. She didn't want to hear her parents' well-meaning advice. She didn't want to think about anything else for a while. And she certainly didn't want to return to class or to her damned doctor's appointment.

She wanted to stretch out on the sofa, but the reminder of 'all things Marty' bothered her too much. Instead, she went to her bedroom and stretched out across her bed. Soon, the meds worked their magic and she lay there floating into a less painful place, a place where her heart was now only a dull ache.

Chapter 10

In the meantime, Becky met Hillary at the Westville Pub for a light dinner and a pint of draft. Becky always enjoyed visiting with her best friend, but she was curious if Hills knew anything about the last body found in the rubble of the recent fire. Twenty residents had lost their lives, but now with Hank, the count had grown to twenty-one. It was a devastating loss for the community.

It didn't make any sense from an investigative view. How had Hank, a resident of Colorado, gotten to those apartments and ended up dead? It certainly wasn't the same address for the residence he'd secured for himself and Lou-Lou, his sister. Although both of the addresses were located in West Asheville, they were miles apart.

"So, what are you working on now?" Hills eagerly asked Becky after the server set down a pint of Pisgah pale ale for each of them.

"A new ghost from the fire last Friday evening," Becky admitted. "Since he didn't live there it's odd that he ended up dead there. Do you have more details about him?"

"Wait, I think I heard his name was Hank Cruz from Colorado. Is that the one you're talking about?"

"That would be him," Becky confirmed.

"What's his deal?" Hills coaxed. "You know I love a good ghost story."

"He says he doesn't remember anything. I was wondering what you knew about it. Has any more details come to light?"

Before Hills could answer, Patty Lawson sashayed over to their table. She wore a black, Daffy Duck cartoon printed box pleated skirt and a yellow and black blouse. The skirt was so full that it flounced as she pranced. Becky and Hills were mesmerized by the skirt – it looked as if Daffy flew towards them.

"Well, if it isn't Pearl and Louie," Patty chortled, referring to the famous interracial couple, Pearl Bailey and Louie Bellson whose marriage had lasted almost forty years.

"As I recall," Hills promptly replied, "They lived a color-blind life, peaceful and content until the day she died. Perhaps you should consider taking a chord or two from their musical score."

Ignoring Hillary's bold but apt comment, Patty glared at Becky. Once she'd seen Becky in the company of Patrick Burns, Patty couldn't let any opportunity slip by without confronting the object of her jealousy.

"So, how's the freak show going, Becky?" Patty asked with a smile plastered on her face and one eyebrow cocked high on her brow. "Are you really sure Patrick is OK with your sideshow?"

"He seems to be quite happy with my ability," Becky reassured as she returned a genuine smile. The mere mention of Patrick's name had that effect on her.

"What's up with your face, Patty? A little too much Botox?" Hills commented as she observed that Patty's eyes were puffy and the eyebrow really did seem to be stuck in the 'up' position. Hills giggled in spite of herself.

Patty Lawless believed that the holy book forbids association with seers and other people who possessed mystical gifts. In her opinion, they should all be considered witches and burned at the stake. Then again, she also believed that it prohibited a lot of other stuff too, such as mixing outside your race and religion. She had always resented and despised that Becky and Hills were best friends.

Patty was rather strict when it came to her religious biases, but rather loose when it came to the men she dated. She'd gone out with Patrick for a short while when they were in college, but he'd quickly broken it off the day she showed up with her packed suitcases expecting to move in with him. He'd finally had to get a restraining order to keep her away, but it wasn't very effective. She simply couldn't let him go.

Noticing with a great deal of envy that Becky had lost a few pounds and looked especially cute in a pair of blue jeans, a blue Henley shirt double-stitched in red, and blue ropers, she quipped, "Lovesick, Becky? Has Patrick consumed your thoughts to the point where you don't even care if you eat? I know the feeling; he once consumed my thoughts too just like I did his."

"Oh, give it a rest, Patty," Becky shot back. "No one cares about your history or escapades. I certainly don't."

"Even if my history is with Patrick?" Patty baited with a coy smile.

"Even then." Becky didn't get caught in the trap.

"Me either," Hills agreed.

"It won't last," Patty declared. "He's rather kinky. You won't be able to keep him satisfied for long. He'll grow tired of your prudish act soon enough."

"He certainly grew tired of your act, Patty," Becky continued to smile sweetly.

"We're not going to get drawn into your drama, Patty. So run along little ducky, run along," Hills chipped in as she waved her fingers in dismissal.

"You two make me sick!" Patty stormed as she pranced away to rejoin her companions.

Chapter 11

"Where were we before that rude interruption?" Becky asked as Hills stared at her with new appreciation.

"I don't know what's changed about you, my friend, but I like it. You aren't as meek and mild-mannered as you used to be. Good for you! Keep it up! We were discussing the coroner's report,"

"That's right," Becky agreed.

"It said Hank Cruz was shot but the cause of death was actually asphyxiation. It stands to reason that he might not have died if he hadn't been there when the fire started. I guess he passed out and didn't wake up in time to move out of harm's way," Hills speculated.

"You've spent too much time with cops, you're beginning to sound like one," Becky teased. "How did you get access to the coroner's report anyway?"

Becky was pleased but a bit amazed. Hillary was a dispatcher and she didn't normally have access to such records. She usually heard and passed on information that came from officers standing around the watercooler as they gossiped about their outcalls.

"Oh," she smiled easily, "I made friends with him in case you ever needed that kind of material. He likes me a lot and we have coffee together on occasion."

"Do you like him a lot?" Becky asked with a grin, hoping it was true. Hills had been about as lucky with men as Becky had been over the years. Neither one of them had been impressed with what was available... until Patrick came along.

"Heck-fire, Becky. He's old, at least in his late forties," Hills southern dialect was more obvious at times. "Besides, he has a wife and two kids. I'm no home-wrecker. I just butter him up a bit to get access to reports, especially if I think it might be of interest to you."

"And I appreciate it very much, Hills."

They stopped talking when the waitress returned with their food order. Becky had selected the Spinach Artichoke Dip which came with chips and warm pita bread. Hills had ordered the Black and Blue Burger which came with fries.

Becky could feel Patty's eyes boring into her when the vegetarian meal arrived. Patty's comment about her weight had not gone unnoticed. Becky was glad that it was obvious she'd lost a couple of pounds. It was certainly better than gaining a few.

"Want some of my fries?" Hills offered.

Becky took one, dipped it in mayonnaise, and took a bite. However, she couldn't take her eyes off the huge blackened burger topped with blue cheese, red onions, and tomatoes that was on its way to Hills mouth. Becky inhaled the aroma that oozed from the massive sandwich. It was so big that Hills grasped it tightly between both hands in an attempt to smash it a bit so she could get a bite. Becky felt faint from hunger.

"What?" Hillary asked with her mouth stuffed with her first huge, juicy bite.

"It looks so good," Becky admitted. "That's what I miss most – hamburgers! Still, even Patty noticed that my vegetarian diet has paid off."

"Why would you care what that twit thinks?"

"I don't care what she thinks, not really. I just don't want to be fat."

"What are you, a size eight?" Hills scoffed. "In what world is that considered fat or overweight? There is nothing wrong with you, Becky Tibbs. Nothing at all. You look healthy and beautiful. Now, stop this foolishness."

"Only because you love me," Becky grinned.

"You want me to cut this burger in half so you can have some?"

"No, not tonight. I'm happy with what I ordered. I just hate to admit that my mother is right… that maybe I should eat meat once or twice a week. She insists it will balance out my moods… and I have been moody lately. I also feel faint sometimes."

"Now, why would you hate to admit that, Becky Tibbs? Our mothers are supposed to give us good advice, right? I mean, it's not like either one of them would tell us to do wrong or say something that would harm us. You hear me? You have to let go of that rubbish."

"I don't know why I feel so upset with Mother or why I can't forgive her for messing up my Thanksgiving dinner," Becky allowed.

"Listen, I know it was a huge disappointment, but it happens – crap happens all the time. My mother pokes her nose in where it doesn't belong too. She's very quick to tell me how even the smallest thing should be done like folding towels or washing dishes. It's almost as if they think there's only one way to do anything. That's just mothers for you. They know best or think they do."

"Yes, but I'm holding a grudge."

"If it makes you feel any better, I once overheard my maternal grandmamma say that life with daughters is like a seesaw, going up and down every ten years or so. Little girls love their mothers when they're under age ten. Then, they're jealous of the woman Daddy loves in their teens. In their twenties, Mama is just an old fool – she can't do anything right and she doesn't know anything. But, the next thing you know, they're thirty and come back around to find that they need their mama now that they have their own kids. In their forties, poor old mama can't do anything right again – and it just occurred to me that it's probably because their own kids are in the teens and hating on them. And finally, when they get to be about fifty and up, they become best friends with their mama again… if they're lucky enough that mama is still around that long."

"Wow!" Becky declared. "I'd love to come up with something profound to say to that, but I'm too stunned and a little worried if that's an accurate assessment. Just wow!"

"It's deep," Hills agreed. "And then, that daughter who gave her mother so much grief gets to experience it all over again with her own daughter. It's a hoot when you really think about how everything comes full circle!"

"Sounds like the cycle of life," Becky agreed.

"Circle, cycle, pretty much the same."

"I guess that applies to me and mom, too. We still have to look forward to that seesaw," Becky worried.

"Probably. Now, what else do you know about this Hank guy?"

Becky filled Hills in on the rest of the information she'd gathered about Hank and his sister before asking, "Does the investigating officer have any ideas about why he was murdered?"

"Well, you have the investigating officer's ear. Why don't you ask him yourself?"

"Patrick has the case?"

"Yep," Hills confirmed.

"I knew he asked me about it this morning when we had coffee, it just didn't register that it was his case."

"That's how it works at the department. The one with the case asks the questions," Hillary grinned. "And, you can discuss it with him all you like. Still, if I hear anything that would be of value, you know you can count on me."

"I know, thanks Hills."

Chapter 12

When Becky got to the shop on Thursday, Jacob was more than a little upset and worried. It was unusual for the helper-ghost to be nervous because normally he was the calmest, most collected ghost in the room. Now, he paced back and forth behind the main counter and uneasily wrung his hands in frustration.

Lois and Myrtle anxiously watched their close friend, feeling helpless and unable to console him.

"What's wrong, Jacob?" Becky quickly asked.

"I can't find Hank."

"Well, you know he didn't cross over yet," Becky soothed. "He wouldn't leave without saying goodbye to his sister."

"I know, but I've found Hank to be very secretive and now this disappearing-act has me concerned."

"Why would that worry you?" Becky asked.

"We were in the process of his education and I was teaching him the things a new ghost needs to know about how to navigate and blink from one place to another. He was making good progress, and then, he disappeared."

"Well, that shows he's a good student."

"Yes, but he left without leaving a trail. It's very worrisome," Jacob fretted.

"He was probably just trying out his new abilities," Becky soothed. "Was that part of your lesson plan? Did you teach him how to *not* leave a trail?"

"Maybe, but not intentionally," Jacob admitted. He knew that Hank wasn't yet ready for that part of the lesson which was similar to trying to learn long division before one had mastered addition and subtraction. It wouldn't do to get things out of order. Now, Jacob wondered if he'd inadvertently given Hank the knowledge he needed for such a task.

This task or 'trick,' as some ghosts called it, was indeed an advantage that more mature ghosts held over newer ghosts. If an immature ghost became a nuisance, an older ghost had an escape plan that enabled him to flee harassment and vengeful spirits who only wanted to cause trouble for others.

Sometimes, a ghost was so angry about his sudden or violent death that he was filled with rage. Such a ghost could cause a lot of problems, not only for the living but also for more peaceful spirits. To effectively avoid those situations, a mature ghost simply blinked straight up into the ethers and then landed somewhere else far away. A new ghost was usually consumed with their own existence and desires. Like a lot of the living, they never thought to look up. Their thinking was more lateral, from side to side and front to back.

"Perhaps he went to see his sister in Pueblo," Lois suggested.

Myrtle nodded in agreement.

"His sister left yesterday," Jacob disagreed. His tone was uncharacteristically sharp.

"But Jacob, it could be true that this has something to do with his sister. Maybe he wanted to make sure she didn't have any trouble on the bus trip."

"I already checked and he didn't go there," Jacob insisted.

"He'll be back," Becky encouraged, not fully understanding Jacob's true worries. "Lou-Lou will arrive in

Asheville tomorrow around four o'clock in the afternoon. He wouldn't miss that."

Jacob thoughtfully nodded, but he wasn't so sure that Hank's disappearance had anything at all to do with Lou-Lou. He was worried that Hank had remembered the darker circumstances surrounding his death. Jacob was troubled that maybe Hank was out for vengeance.

Jacob wasn't ready to involve Becky just yet, but he considered that he might need her advice soon. Before his disappearance, Hank had muttered a phrase that was very disturbing to the senior ghost. He'd claimed, "I died for nothing."

If Hank had recalled his murder and the name of the person responsible, then he might be planning his revenge right now. Jacob was aware that ghosts were incapable of actual murder; they couldn't wield the proper tools to kill someone. Heck, they couldn't even make a phone call. That's where Becky came in. Alive, she could do the physical things required to help a ghost with their unfinished business. But, that didn't mean they couldn't affect events and circumstances that would lead to someone's death.

By causing enough chaos and fear, they were able to trigger a person into doing something foolish that would get them seriously injured and maybe killed. Such tactics could cause a person to drive too fast, trip on an uneven sidewalk, or fall over a concrete ledge. He certainly didn't want a murder on his conscience if there was any way at all to stop it. But, for now, he hoped for the best and felt that he could only wait and see.

Chapter 13

When Marty returned to work on Friday, he was in the foulest possible mood and he took his anguish out on anyone and everyone that got in his way... and it seemed that everything and everyone did get in his way.

He slammed doors. He kicked chairs and trash cans. He angrily raked his desk scattering papers and files across the floor.

His assistant quickly glanced into his office, but when she spied the mess he'd created, she quickly turned away, muttering, "Don't expect me to clean that up."

He was like a bull charging around a corral looking for something or someone to gore, to hurt. His reaction to any inconvenience was blazing hot and over the top.

Soon, everyone in his department avoided him and tried to stay clear of him, but it didn't really help. He was damned and determined to take out his frustration and rage on someone... and anyone would do.

When he learned that another body had been found at the burned-out apartment buildings while he was away and that Patrick Burns had the case, he fumed. Knowing that the detective would be in contact with Becky Tibbs, the thought thoroughly irked him. Even the name 'Tibbs' disgusted him now.

Barbara's face that had regularly flitted through his mind for the last fifteen years, bringing a smile in its wake, now sent shivers of hatred through this soul.

He called Patrick in for the latest information.

Patrick, unaware of Marty's change of heart, candidly shared what he'd learned about the body from Becky along with the coroner's report.

"What's dead should stay dead!" Marty blasted. "I'm sick of this 'dead people walking and talking' crap. I can't believe that you buy into this bullshit!"

"Now, hold on Sergeant," Patrick argued. "You're the one who told me that Becky had a special ability. You even told me that she helped you solve a cold case some time back. You personally know what she can do. How can you suddenly believe that what Becky does is 'crap?' Are you all right? What's gotten into you?"

"Well, I was confused," Marty hedged at first, seemingly unsure about his new opinion for the moment. He knew that what Patrick said was true – he had believed in the girl until yesterday. The scene with Barbara replayed in his mind and he felt the hurt all over again. His voice rose in volume until he was shouting. "Now, I see this bullshit for what it is. I've changed my mind and, as an officer of the law under my command, I suggest you do the same!"

Patrick knew better than to argue with a senior officer, even when that person was wrong, but he also understood his rights. No one could tell him who to trust or with whom he could keep company, especially when he was off the job.

He was stunned at the changes in Marty, but he held his tongue. This was a new development, but there had to be an underlying reason for the differences he'd noticed in his sergeant. Patrick didn't think he could wait until their dinner tonight to let Becky know about this. He really wanted her opinion and advice about the changes he'd just witnessed.

After their meeting, Marty stormed around the department looking for anyone else he could rail on. He spied Hillary on the phone and stomped over to her. She stopped talking to give him her attention but hadn't disconnected the call.

"I understand that you give Becky Tibbs updates that are strictly confidential police business...," Marty began his new rant as he shook a finger at the dispatcher.

"No. Not strictly confidential stuff, but I do talk to her," Hillary interrupted. She was incensed at his tone and the insinuated accusation he made. And, to wag a finger at her like she was a child! How dare he do such a thing!

"This is your only warning, Miss Sweetwater. If I catch you doing that again, if I even see you meeting with her again, you can kiss this job goodbye! Do I make myself clear?" he stormed.

"I may work at the police department, but *you* are *not* my supervisor. You can't tell me who my friends are, Sergeant Smith!" Hillary stood and shouted back. "Becky Tibbs has been my best friend since kindergarten. If it ever comes between a job and her, then I choose Becky! Do I make myself clear?"

So far, Marty had gotten away with his unbridled outburst. Hillary was the first and only person to call him on it. He stepped back a bit when her fiery reply hit him in the face.

Although she was shaking inside, Hillary's voice was loud and clear. She wanted to make sure that everyone in the place heard her. She could only hope that it got back to the Chief. It wasn't often that there were rows and noisy quarrels inside the departmental walls, however, when it did happen, the Chief found out about them. Somehow she didn't think the Chief of Police would be too pleased with Marty Smith's unorthodox demands.

Even though Becky had hoped for a small, intimate dinner with Patrick, after he'd called to tell her the things Marty had said, she placed a call to Barbara first and then to Bobby insisting that they join her at the family home that evening. Only moments after she'd finished the call with Bobby, Hillary called.

Hills divulged the disturbing ultimatum Marty Smith had given her. Becky invited Hillary to dinner too, saying, "We all need to share what we know with each other before this gets completely out of hand."

"I think we're too late for that, Becks. That man is on a warpath and he's going to run over anyone who stands in his way... Did you say that Barbara and Bobby will also be there? And Patrick... he'll be there too?"

"Everyone will be there. Don't be late."

Chapter 14

In the meantime, Jacob had finally caught up with Hank at a motel near the I-40 and I-240 interchange. Hank was so involved in tormenting his stepdad that he didn't notice the helper ghost.

Joey Ramírez was a hard man. His features were severe and rough. His body was thick and rigid. He barely stood five feet nine, but he gave the impression that he was a much larger force, inflexible, callous, and unfeeling. Jacob's father, long dead now, would have described Joey as 'hard as nails and twice as sharp.'

Joey's dark, hooded eyes darted around the motel room – he knew something was there. As an enforcer for the cartel, his perceptions and intuition had been finely honed to pick up the slightest emotional inconsistencies in those who found themselves on the outs with his feared employer. Joey could sense the anger around him even if he couldn't see it.

Some 'thing' was after him. Whatever it was caused the static disturbances in his motel room. That scared him even more.

The horror stories his old, creepy Abuela had told him years ago returned to him. As her wrinkled, leathery face had maliciously contorted in a devilish grimace to drive the story home, she'd filled his head with tales of ghosts and ghouls that came for wicked, evil men. She'd warned him to grow-up good, but he hadn't listened. He'd become so wicked that his reputation reached the ear of the cartel. As a result, they had enlisted him as their primary battering ram. Joey was the one called when someone went astray or tried to cheat his bosses. He was respected and feared for the terror his name instilled.

Joey knew he was morally evil. Under orders, he'd tortured and killed many men and women. Now, he'd just shot his stepson; he'd mercilessly tried to kill Hank. As far as Joey knew, the boy could be bleeding out in some alley right now. But, he honestly didn't feel guilty about that. It was a dog-eat-dog world and his own survival depended on Hank's demise. Still, Joey sensed that what he'd done to his stepson was somehow pivotal in this spooky harassment he now suffered.

"Perhaps this evil tormentor knows I also plan to do the same to my stepdaughter when she arrives," he thought.

Joey reflected on how difficult it had been to hurt Louise in the past. It wasn't due to his lack of desire, but it had never worked out. She'd always had a strong defense and protection surrounding her. Oh, he'd beaten and cursed her often enough. He'd reviled and hated her too, but there was always something that prevented him from abusing his stepdaughter the way he really wanted. Perhaps this nasty ghoul that tormented him knew his darkest secrets and his dirty desires.

Jacob uneasily watched as Hank caused all manner of mischief and chaos. First, he caused the lights to flicker. Then, the television turned on and off. Next, he turned over the trash basket and knocked lamps off end tables. It was enough to scare the living daylights out of anyone in their right mind.

It was working; Joey Ramírez quaked in terror as everything in his duffle bag spilled out onto the floor. Jacob observed the contents. There had to be thousands of dollars in the pile, all tightly wrapped and bound in neat bundles.

No one carried around money like that unless they were up to something bad.

Jacob was distracted by that consideration, but Hank wasn't even close to finished. Next, used towels flew through the air and landed in Joey's face along with any toiletries that sat on the vanity. The pointed end of the toothbrush scarcely missed his eye. The razor was next and the blades nicked his left ear. Joey threw up his hand to block a small bottle of aftershave that flew towards his head.

Suddenly, Joey didn't want to wait for Lou-Lou's arrival. Now, all he wanted to do was get away from this evil, to run as fast as he could.

"Run, and get the hell out of Dodge," his self-preservation urged. *"Run back to your life in Pueblo."*

But, Joey knew he couldn't do that empty-handed. He needed to find Hank's body and the property the little bastard had stolen. He couldn't go back empty-handed or he'd pay for the crime himself.

The cartel was unforgiving.

Jacob and Hank were ghosts, not mind readers. Neither knew the heavy and dark thoughts that consumed Joey Ramírez. They certainly didn't know the true details of the money or that Joey assumed Hank was still alive. It was difficult to imagine that the seemingly powerful man who stood before them was actually tormented by the tall-tales he'd heard as a child.

Feeling some sympathy for Joey, Jacob blinked directly in front of Hank in an effort to stop him.

"You must stop this insanity, Hank," Jacob insisted.

"You don't understand," Hank replied. "I died for nothing. Absolutely nothing! It was a senseless waste. He simply couldn't let me and Lou-Lou leave to find happiness elsewhere."

"If your stepdad is from Pueblo, how did he come to be in Asheville?"

"He followed me here. He followed me here to make sure we didn't get any peace or a happily ever after. That's what Lou-Lou always dreamed about, a 'happily-ever-after.' Someplace away from this horrible bastard."

"How did he know you'd be here?" Jacob inquired in an effort to get Hank to think it through.

"He beat it out of Lou-Lou."

"Why do you think that?" Jacob asked.

"Because when I saw her on the bus, she was black and blue. A black eye, bruises on her arms, and her ear was nearly torn off her head."

"What?" Jacob croaked. Shock quickly replaced the sympathy he'd previously felt for Joey.

"Yeah, this sorry excuse for a stepfather liked to grab us by the ears and drag us to our rooms. He said it made us listen to him." Hanks's voice grew harshly bitter as he recalled the abuse he and his sister had suffered.

"I still don't understand, Hank. How did he get here so quickly, even before your sister?"

"Isn't it obvious?" Hank conceded indicating the pile of money. "Money is no object for him. He caught a flight and then rented a car."

"OK, so he followed you here, but why did he shoot you? How would that benefit him? Didn't he want to force you to return home? And, where did he get that pile of cash?" Jacob asked as he tried to understand this senseless tragedy.

"How the hell do I know? He's Joey Ramirez, the enforcer for the cartel. Who knows where it came from and who knows why this happened to me. Your guess is as good as mine. Mainly, he's just bad news, a sorry piece of crap!" Hank bellowed before he blinked away.

Jacob now knew more than he'd known earlier, but it wasn't enough. He also knew that he had to get Becky involved even though Joey was a dangerous man. She was so talented at figuring out the angles behind this type of vengeance that he really needed her help now.

He also knew that she had a lot on her plate. He'd overheard the call with Patrick and the ensuing calls to Barbara and Bobby. Jacob didn't know everything said, but he'd heard enough to know that something was up with Marty Smith that could affect all their lives.

He also knew that Becky would pick up Lou-Lou at the bus station this afternoon. Jacob hoped that Lou-Lou's presence would calm Hank and bring him back to some semblance of sanity, but after what he'd just witnessed, he couldn't count on that happening. Once a ghost had gone off the rails, it was very difficult to steer him back on a righteous course.

When Jacob returned to the shop, Becky saw that he was still distressed about Hank. "Talk to me, Jacob. I know you well enough to know when something's bothering you. Spill it."

Jacob told Becky everything that had worried him earlier. He told her that now he knew for sure his concerns were founded. That Hank was torturing his stepdad. The two of them discussed the situation at some length and then made a plan.

After their extensive conversation ended, Becky closed the shop early for the evening and then went to pick up Lou-Lou from the bus station.

Jacob returned to the motel to keep an eye on Joey Ramírez.

He worried that Joey had remained in town because he waited for Lou-Lou to arrive. Perhaps, he also wanted to kill her. The thought was disturbing and that's why Jacob couldn't let the man out of his sight. He had to make sure that no one else died.

Even with everything going on in Becky's life, Jacob trusted that she would untangle the mess once she had everyone together. And, he wanted to make sure she was able to carry out her plan.

Everything depended on Becky.

It was a lot to ask of anyone.

Chapter 15

At dinner that night, Barbara, Bobby, Patrick, and Hillary gathered around the dining room table with Becky to eat. Since she hadn't had time to cook a meal, Becky had picked up a complete dinner from Earth Fare's deli.

Now, as she observed those congregated around her table, she was pleased to see that the ready-made food was enough to feed the crowd. Since everyone was friends or family, it was a casual meeting, but the atmosphere grew tense as they each began to share snippets of individual stories about Marty Smith.

Bobby hadn't seen Marty that day and didn't have anything to add, but he carefully watched Barb's reaction as the others made a few comments about Marty going off the rails at work. After a couple of minutes, he finally, held up his hand, "Whoa, whoa, now. Everyone, let's hear what Barbara has to say. I bet she has some insight into how this got started."

Reluctantly, Barb began to tell her story. She gave the details about Marty's visit to her apartment in Raleigh the day before and their breakup. Her enlightening and emotional specifics shed the most light on the reasons the Sergeant had a burr up his lower, most tender regions.

Always the clown of the family, and after hearing his sister's tearful tale, Bobby loudly exclaimed, "He's butt-hurt!" His jovial summation caused laughter around the table, but the mood quickly turned serious again.

"He dumped me!" Barbara proclaimed. "I'm the one who should feel hurt. I guess that's why I kept the secret from him for so long. Somehow I knew he'd react this way."

"You must feel terrible, Barb. I'm so sorry," Becky consoled.

"Wait," Hills interrupted, "do you mean that you see ghosts too? That's the big secret that you shared with Marty Smith?"

"She does and so do I," Bobby cackled. "Helluva thing, isn't it?"

Hills turned accusing eyes to Becky, "You didn't think that was important enough to clue me in?"

"It was their secret to share, Hills," Becky said. "We each agreed years ago that we'd deal with our gifts the way we thought best and as necessary. Mine became public knowledge, but Bobby and Barb didn't feel the same way. They've chosen to remain in the closet for the most part."

"A choice," Barbara added as she dabbed her eyes.

"Did he really say he thought we should be locked up?" Becky gulped with disbelief as she turned back to her sister. Barb nodded that it was true. "I can't believe it. He knows that the thing with Josh was real. He had the glass on his shirt to prove it. He arrested Josh's father."

"Not to mention a few cuts on his face," Bobby added with a chuckle. "Man-oh-man, this gets more and more bizarre."

Once again, his joking response lightened the mood for a moment, until Patrick solemnly added, "He thinks it's all a bunch of crap now. He doesn't want me to consult with Becky about anything that could be ghost-related or police-related."

"Same here!" Hills echoed. "But, I've got news for Mr. High and Mighty Marty Smith, he can't tell me who I can be friends with. I'll go straight to the Chief if I have to!"

"Aren't you related to the Chief?" Patrick asked.

"Yeah, but that's not why he'll listen to me. He likes me. He personally hired me because of my excellent scores, not because he's married to my second cousin," Hills explained.

"This is some tangled up complication!" Bobby groaned. "And, all because Barbara finally told him the truth. Didn't you tell him he wouldn't have to worry about it because you take meds to block it, Barb?"

"It dinna matter," Barb slurred as the wine and too many meds began to kick in. "I honestly believe he'd already made up his mind about us before we talked about everything. Somehow he'd already figured it out before I could tell him."

"It's always worse if they hear it through the grapevine instead of directly from the horse's mouth. I wonder who told him," Bobby asked as he glanced at Patrick.

"Don't look at me," Patrick defended. "I didn't know that you or Barbara had the same gift as Becky."

"It probably had something to do with Becky's latest ghost adventure and kidnapping then," Bobby said, eliciting a smile from Hillary.

Chapter 16

"Why did you wait so long to tell him?" Patrick asked. Barbara flinched at the question, and one look at her crestfallen expression, caused him to hurriedly add, "I'm sorry and I'm not judging you. It's just that you and Marty were a couple and couples don't normally keep secrets from each other." His gaze traveled to Becky and she nodded and smiled at him extracting a dimpled grin in response.

"I suppose that I knew from the beginning that he wouldn't be able to accept it or take the heat of it."

"Take the heat?" Bobby interrupted.

"You have to understand that Marty has to have acceptance from his peers and fellow officers. It's just who he is. He goes along with and supports popular beliefs that don't challenge those ideals. Marty is heavily influenced by the opinions of others."

Becky heard Zetmeh add,

A weeping willow leans and changes
direction as the wind blows.

"It's almost as if he needs that to feel normal," Barb continued. "I guess I knew the truth of my gift would end whatever we had and I didn't want to lose him. I shouldn't be shocked because I knew it was coming. I knew it all too well. I've said way too much already. I think my lips are really loose."

A Medium's Christmas Gift

Bobby noticed his parents standing behind Barbara as they tried to console her, but Barb was unaware of their presence. Unable to handle the grief and disappointment from the breakup, she'd taken a few extra Xanax after Marty left and a few extra today as well. The extra meds combined with the two or three glasses of wine at dinner had very effectively blocked them.

Bobby hadn't drunk enough yet to block them, but he'd still drunk enough to be agitated by their uninvited presence. His ears perked up nicely when he overheard Joyce whisper, "I told you, honey, if you knew the things we know about Marty Smith, you'd be glad he was out of your life. Count yourself lucky, my dear. Simply count yourself very lucky indeed."

"Then enlighten us, Mom," Bobby requested. "Tell us why Barb should be glad Marty dumped her."

"Don't take that tone with your mother, Son," Justin cautioned.

Immediately chagrined by his father, Bobby mumbled a low apology, "Sorry, Mom."

"I heard you too, Mom. It might help all of us if you just spilled the beans and told us what you know," Becky added.

Hills and Patrick were truly dumbfounded at the half conversation – they couldn't keep up. And, even though Hills and Patrick had both seen Becky in action when she'd talked to ghosts, it was usually prefaced with, "He's here now." Becky hadn't indicated that a ghost was present at this time and they knew they were missing something important.

"Wait, you guys," Hillary interrupted. "Who are you talking to now?"

Justin Tibbs immediately saw the inherent dangers and counseled, "This is a topic that should be discussed amongst family members only and certainly not in public. Joyce, let's go. Barbara can't hear or see us anyway."

"All right, Justin. Hold your horses," Joyce replied. "Just let me talk to Becky for a minute. Becky, I'm really happy that you're talking to me again. Does this mean that you're no longer mad at me? Can I stop by tomorrow to chat with you?"

"I suppose so," Becky agreed.

"Then, we'll continue this in the morning," Bobby insisted, "because you do need to fill us in. Marty Smith is determined to ruin Becky's life if he can. We might need a little ammunition. See you in the morning, Mom."

Becky agreed but added, "I don't know why you won't tell us now. You know that Hills is practically family and I don't keep secrets from Patrick."

"Your mother will see you and Bobby alone in the morning," Justin barked, indicating that was the end of the discussion.

Becky smiled at Hills and Patrick as she admitted, "My folks just dropped by to check on Barbara. But, my sister took too many Xanax and didn't even notice they were here. They're gone now. And Patrick, we need to get over to Lou-Lou's new apartment. Jacob is waiting on us," she reminded him.

"Y'all go on and do your thing," Hills grudgingly agreed.

"We will," Becky smiled.

She hadn't been fooled for even a second about the unseen visitors. From the things Bobby had said, something big was up. She was damned if she'd be left out of the loop.

"I'm going to sit here with Bobby and Barbara for a while and have a cold one or two. Besides, from the looks of your sister, I might need to help Bobby tuck Barbara in bed pretty soon."

Becky glanced at Barb and could see it was true.

Barb loved her wine and she'd had too much at dinner which probably would've been fine if that was all she'd had. She was now dazed and confused.

"You might want to go ahead and do that," Becky advised. "See everyone later."

Becky left with Patrick and Hills was happy to have time with Bobby.

Chapter 17

Earlier that afternoon, and after Becky had picked up Lou-Lou from the bus station, she'd taken Hank's sister to the furnished apartment he'd rented for them. It was a real shame that he'd never get to live there.

When they had arrived at the address Hank had provided, Becky and Lou-Lou were amazed to discover the new apartment was actually a small cottage located on private, wooded acreage. Each small home was nestled in its own grove of trees, giving the illusion of solitude even though it was a tiny community.

Being a seasonal rental, the cottage was fully stocked with everything a guest would need, including cookware, dishes, utensils, towels, and linens.

"It has everything you need, Lou-Lou, except a toothbrush and food," Becky commented.

Hank had rented the small cabin for a period of three months. He'd thought that such a short lease would give them time to look around Asheville, find a job, and then, find a regular, more permanent place to live.

Knowing that Lou-Lou had her heart set on a house with a yard, this small cottage had a cute little backyard with a nice covered patio. That patch of earth was the main feature that had sold Hank on such a temporary solution to their living arrangements.

He knew his sister would love it… and she did.

A Medium's Christmas Gift

Becky had helped Lou-Lou get her two extra-large duffle bags, purse, and backpack inside, and then, they took a moment to look around. The front entrance opened into a smaller than normal living room that contained a sofa and one armchair, a tall bookcase, and a T.V. stand that held a newer model flat screen television and a DVD player. A few movies and books were stacked on the bookcase. The sofa and matching armchair were ably upholstered in a wide, brown and red plaid that gave the room a cheerful atmosphere.

The two bedrooms were very small also, just large enough to accommodate a full-size bed and a nightstand with a lamp. The beds were made up with matching patchwork quilts. It looked very homey and welcoming, but Becky noticed that the closet would have to do for both hanging and folded clothing. The room was too small for a chest of drawers or dresser.

A full bathroom was located between the bedrooms. It held a shower and tub combination with sliding doors, a toilet, and a small vanity with a mirrored medicine cabinet hanging above it. The cabinet held travel-size toiletries that would allow the guest time to pick up their own.

The kitchen was galley style, with all appliances provided, including a washer-slash-dryer combination. The kitchen stretched across the full length of the cottage with a small dinette set at the opposite end and a sliding door that led to the patio.

"It looks as if it has everything a person could need," Becky acknowledged. "Hank did very well to find this place so quickly."

"Oh, I love it!" Lou-Lou joyfully exclaimed. "It's just perfect! Look at the backyard. It's perfect too. I can sit out there in peace and read while I drink a glass of tea."

"Or a cup of hot cocoa in this weather," Becky cheerfully suggested as an alternative. She thoughtfully gazed at Lou-Lou. "Being from Colorado, you're used to cold weather, right?"

"Of course, but I suspect that since you get the four seasons here, it will be different and maybe not as cold. In our part of the world, it often felt as if we only had two seasons – spring and winter."

"It does get cold here, but not as severe as what you're used to dealing with there. We can even get a little snow on occasion. You brought plenty of warm clothes?"

"I did and oh, how I wish I could thank Hank in person for this!"

"Well, don't give up on that just yet," Becky soothed. "I'm hoping that you can thank him too."

Becky had also asked Patrick to find Hank's car earlier in the day. With Lou-Lou's description, his search was successful and he'd driven the car to Becky's that night.

Presently, Patrick followed Becky to Lou-Lou's cottage. He wasn't sure what would happen next, but Becky had assured him that he would see ghost activity.

He secretly hoped he was up for the challenge.

While Patrick drove behind her, Becky watched him in her rearview mirror. She didn't know what she'd done to deserve someone so sweet and caring, so attentive to her needs, and so accepting of her ability, but her heart filled with emotion as she thought about how extremely joyful and thankful she was that she had. She was astonished that their care and affection for each other had happened so quickly and naturally too.

It was cosmic, my dear one, simply cosmic, Zetmeh acknowledged.

Becky also felt sick when she considered the way things had ended for Barbara and Marty. They'd had years to get to know each other… and they hadn't even bothered to share the most important aspects of their lives. *"Look how that turned out,"* she silently scoffed. *"I vow to never keep secrets from Patrick."*

Becky felt quite miserable when she thought of the loss each one of them now suffered. Marty was already showing the battle scars. It was eating him up. Then she worried, *"Will Barbara turn bitter and hateful too?"*

It was perplexing to Becky. She'd never been in love or had a relationship like the one she now had with Patrick. But even this small taste of it made her certain that she didn't want it to end, especially the way her sister's relationship with Marty had ended. Becky began to have more sympathy for her sister, *"No wonder she kept her gift a secret. If she knew he couldn't accept it, she had no other option than to keep it from him... especially since she loved him and didn't want to lose him. Oh, it just sucks!"*

Zetmeh's soothing voice whispered,

> *They never really knew each other, my dear. Barbara kept the most intimate part of herself hidden from a man who didn't want to see or know the beautiful woman she truly had become. It isn't the same for you and Patrick. He accepts all there is about you. He knows how special you are and he loves you.*

"I hope you're right," Becky responded.

Chapter 18

Patrick parked Hank's car at Lou-Lou's new place under the small overhang that served as a carport. Then, he and Becky went inside for a moment to give her an update. After introducing Patrick, Becky said, "Lou-Lou, listen carefully. Your stepdad, Joey Ramírez, is in town. We have reason to believe that he's responsible for Hank's death."

"Joey is here!" Lou-Lou wailed fearfully at the news and, in her anguish, she nearly fell to the floor.

Patrick caught her and led her to the sole armchair. "Don't be afraid, Lou-Lou. I'm a police officer. You're safe and I'll get to the bottom of this. I promise."

Inconsolable, Lou-Lou continued to cry a high-pitched keening sound that jangled their nerves and caused Becky to fret. Although the cabins were situated several yards apart for privacy, Becky worried that a neighbor might overhear the unusual uproar and call the cops. The racket she made certainly sounded as if someone was horribly tortured or dying.

"We're going to the motel to speak to Joey Ramírez now," Becky tried to talk over Lou-Lou's lamentations. She hoped to distract Lou-Lou from the storm that consumed her. "Please, don't be afraid. We'll get the information we need and come back as soon as we're done. Patrick will arrest Joey and he'll never be able to hurt you again."

Lou-Lou still howled as if none of it mattered.

A Medium's Christmas Gift

In an attempt to give the young woman hope, Becky encouraged, "Hank will be with us when we return. I'm sure he has a lot to say to you, so please don't worry or be sad. Try to relax. Maybe you could put on a heavy coat and enjoy a cup of hot tea or cocoa on the patio until we return? Joey doesn't know where you live and you really are safe. Please, Lou, don't cry."

Becky knew she was babbling, but she was grasping for something that would soothe the girl and stop her loud, eerie sorrow. It was unsettling and her ears hurt from it. She'd worked with many angry ghosts, but she didn't have the experience needed when working with a living human being, especially one as tormented as Louise. She looked to Patrick for help, but he was as bumfuzzled as she was.

He'd dealt with a lot of grieving victims and their survivors, but he'd never encountered such loud, vociferous sorrow or fear. Still, he gave it his best effort too, "Come on, Lou, don't you trust us? We told you that I'll get a confession and arrest Joey for the murder of Hank. Things can only get better for you."

"You don't understand," Lou-Lou finally used her words and cried out, "I told Joey where Hank would be. I'm the one responsible for my brother's death. If I hadn't given in, Hank would still be alive."

"From the looks of your face, you didn't have much choice," Patrick gently allowed. "Looks like he beat you up pretty badly."

Lou-Lou halted her loud crying for a moment and used the sleeve of her blouse to wipe at the tears streaming down her face. Becky took that cue and went to the small bathroom. She brought back a long length of tissue paper and handed it to the girl.

"I still told Joey that Hank was in Asheville. Why didn't I think to point him in a different direction? Why did I tell him the truth? If I had only lied, but I didn't I caved in and told him the truth. Hank is now dead because of me.

Nothing you can say will change that." The noisy wailing started again, but Patrick firmly grasped Lou's shoulder.

"Stop, Lou. Just stop," Patrick demanded. His stern voice finally broke through her tearful haze, "Your brother is dead because your stepfather killed him. Don't put that burden anywhere except where it belongs."

Lou-Lou wiped away the tears that had stopped as suddenly as they'd started.

"Will you be all right until we get back, Lou? We really need to go now," Becky urged as she anxiously glanced at her watch. Calming Hank's sister had taken a large bite out of their schedule. They were supposed to meet with Jacob almost half-an-hour earlier. She knew that he'd be concerned at their delay.

"I'll be fine," Lou calmly assured. The storm had finally passed and both Becky and Patrick were equally relieved. "Just please, be careful, Joey is really bad news. It's his job to hurt people and he likes doing it."

Chapter 19

Patrick and Becky left with a promise to return as soon as possible. They took Becky's truck and, as they continued on their way, neither of them mentioned Lou-Lou's bizarre meltdown or her method of displaying her grief. They still struggled to understand it and put it in the past.

They arrived at the small Mom and Pop motel in less than half an hour. The parking lot was filled with work trucks. Some of the trucks had mounted iron racks and some had huge toolboxes that filled their truck beds.

Apparently, the rooms were frequented by construction guys who were trying to save money when working away from home.

It wasn't the nicest option in town or the worst – it was merely an option. Nonetheless, just as it had served the purposes of the electricians, plumbers, carpenters, and crane operator occupants it had also served Joey Ramirez's needs. He required an inexpensive and out of the way base to lay low and remain unnoticed while he carried out his dirty work.

When Patrick and Becky approached Joey's room number, it was eerily quiet and dark. They wondered if Joey was even there. However, Jacob had been waiting for them to arrive and was quickly by Becky's side to let her know what was going on inside.

"Hank has destroyed all the lights except those built into the ceiling," Jacob advised. "Joey appears terrified. He stands in the corner of the room, praying or cursing in a language I don't know. Perhaps it's Spanish. I can't be sure. If he was a ghost, there is no language barrier and I could tell you what he is saying, but I can't make it out."

"What's Hank doing?"

"Anything he can to keep Joey scared, but he knows you are here now so he has stopped for the time being. He left earlier and was gone for a few minutes; I assumed it was to check on his sister's arrival. This situation is truly terrible, Becky. I'm sorry I got you into this."

"Don't apologize, Jacob. We help ghosts. Hank needs help. Does Joey have a gun?" she asked, concerned for Patrick's safety.

"I haven't seen one, but if he did have a gun, as scared as he is, he'd have probably pulled it out before now." Jacob realized the absurdity of the situation and chuckled softly before adding, "It's crazy, Becky. But, I guess it's better to laugh than to cry."

Becky wanted to tell Jacob that he'd never seen crying until he'd see the spine-tingling racket Lou-Lou could make, but before she could say any more, Patrick banged on the door, "Police! Open up," he shouted.

When Joey answered the door, he was actually glad to see the police officer standing there. Even though Patrick wasn't in uniform, he held out his badge to identify himself as such. Patrick was surprised that the man met him with such relief, until Becky whispered, "He's been abused and terrorized by a ghost all day. It's understandable that he is grateful to see you."

Sweaty with the acrid smell of fear, Joey's entire body shook with trepidation. He held out his hands with wrists crossed, "Here," he pleaded, "Cuff me. Arrest me. Lock me up. Maybe then I'll be free from this hellhound after me."

"Hellhound?" Becky muttered in surprise. She'd never before heard a ghost called that.

"Something's after you?" Patrick coughed, trying to hide his surprise that there were 'just deserts' after all. He'd often wondered if people ever got what they deserved. If something was truly after this man, then, it was more than likely justified. "Are you Joey Ramírez from Pueblo, Colorado?"

"Yes, I am. Are you here to arrest me?"

"I'm Detective Patrick Burns and this is Becky Tibbs. We're here to question you about your stepson, Hank Cruz. May we come in?" Patrick replied, loath to give anything away just yet.

Joey stood back against the door and gestured that they should enter. At this point, he didn't yet know if Hank had filed a police complaint, but it was something that his bitch of a stepson would do if he had the opportunity. Joey considered that he'd wounded Hank pretty badly. He hadn't expected him to recover so quickly if at all. But with the advances in modern medicine, he knew it was possible.

Joey also knew the law and he understood that ultimately, his attack on Hank was attempted murder. He could only assume that was why they were here.

He glanced at Becky and made a quick assessment. She certainly wasn't 'po-po' or this dude's partner on the job. Before he could wonder more about her he found himself distracted by the real cop.

Patrick went in first and located the light switches, turning them on. Once the few remaining lights were on, Becky cautiously entered the room. She saw that Jacob was now standing beside Hank and neither one of the ghosts looked very happy.

"Turning on the lights won't make any difference. Whatever is here will make them crackle and sputter again before they go out. It might even cause them to explode or it might throw a lamp or bash it on the dresser." Joey's voice was flat and hopeless.

Becky and Patrick took in the details of the motel room. It was a disastrous wreck. Everything was thrown around – one mattress was off its frame, the bedding and sheets were stripped from the beds, clean and dirty towels were added to the mix, and empty food containers were littered across the floor.

In spite of all that, Patrick ignored Joey's tired warnings. He encouraged Joey to sit at the small table situated before the wide windows that overlooked the parking lot. Then, he pulled out the only other chair for Becky. Finally, without another option, Patrick sat on the edge of the remaining rumpled bed.

Chapter 20

"Did you kill Hank Cruz?" Patrick bluntly asked.

"I shot him, but I didn't know he was dead," Joey slowly responded. The forceful query made him cautious. A murder charge was a lot different than an attempted murder indictment. He hadn't expected it.

"He's dead," Patrick announced.

"I wasn't sure," Joey repeated and, as he carefully considered his options, his eyes returned to the girl that was with the police officer. He considered that he could easily overpower the man and take the woman hostage. He also knew he'd have to kill her once he made his escape. But, as he looked at Becky Tibbs, he knew there was something odd about her. Something strange and almost inexplicable.

Before he could figure out more, the young redhead sat up straight, closed her dazzling blue eyes, and tuned him out. As if performing some kind of ritual, she had blocked his probing examination.

Joey was stunned. No one had ever been able to keep him out, to prevent him from using his keen instincts to examine their character. The fact that she did such a thing so easily sent a chill down his spine.

"Your stepson, Hank Cruz is here, Joey," Becky remarked after a few moments of silence.

"What? Where?" Joey yelled. "I don't believe you!"

Becky looked at Hank and encouraged, "Tell me something that only you know about your stepfather."

"He's a dog that works for the cartel," Hank replied, and I bet he stole all that money in his duffle bag from them. He married my mother when I was six years old and got her hooked on crack when I was thirteen. He's a dirty, rotten bastard who beat the crap out of Lou-Lou to find out where I had gone."

Becky repeated most of what Hank had said, but she decided not to mention anything about money just yet. She watched Joey carefully for his reaction. His eyes grew even wider as the reality hit home.

Becky often got that response from the living when she shared the details that only a ghost could know. She could only imagine that the effects of Hank's words had made Joey a believer, but she didn't know the half of it.

Although it was true that Joey accepted the message as true, he also realized that this sweet, innocent-looking girl was actually a powerful she-devil. She had to be to possess such command. Once again, he felt helpless and confused as he saw his chances to flee dissipate. He knew that if he tried to take her hostage, she'd be protected. He'd be jumping from the frying pan into the fire. Finally, after running through every possibility, Joey gave up.

"He's really here," Joey stated. His voice was flat, almost listless. "He was throwing things around earlier… He's the ghost or ghoul terrorizing me. My Abuela warned me about such things but I thought she was an old, crazy bitch that didn't know anything. He's here to seek revenge and make me pay for his death." Joey seemed resolute in all that he said as if nothing mattered anymore and Becky had no idea that her presence was responsible for his change of heart.

"So, you did kill him?" Patrick, ready for a confession, interjected.

"I shot him. I suppose he died from that."

"What do you mean?" Patrick asked.

A Medium's Christmas Gift

"I didn't see him die, but if he's dead I guess it was from my doing – from my gunshot," Joey said. "A .45 leaves a big exit hole."

"Why did you shoot him?" Becky asked. "What did you possibly have to gain from his death? He only wanted to start a new life with Louise, to get away from your abuse and the terrible drug racket in Pueblo."

"What he said is true," Joey admitted as if he hadn't heard Becky's last questions. "His description of our family relationship is accurate. I did those things. But, what he doesn't know is that the money I stole from the cartel was intended to give his mother a better life away from Pueblo. We had a place picked out in southern Texas, close to our relatives in Mexico. It's already paid for and waiting on our arrival. That's not going to happen now."

"No, it's not," Patrick said. "You will face murder charges. Maybe your wife can enjoy that plan, but you won't."

"If they find out it was me, they will peel the skin off my feet and kill my family. They'll make me watch that before they kill me." His face contorted as he accepted the reality and foolishness of the unforgivable crime he'd committed against his bosses,

"Hank knows about the money," Becky admitted.

"Then he should understand that to kill him seemed like the only thing to do at the time. I could take his body back and blame him for the missing money. It might've caused his mother some grief, but it would've saved her life. They'll kill us both now." Joey laughed bitterly and then said, "You see, when Hank ran away, he made himself the perfect scapegoat. He made it easy to pin the theft on him."

"Spell it out for me, please," Becky coaxed. She knew that in order to successfully help Hank after they were done with Joey, she'd need as much information as possible. However, with Patrick a police officer, he already knew the answers to what Becky wanted to know. He saw the picture forming easily. Still, he didn't interrupt and allowed Becky to ask her questions without interference.

"When the money went missing, as an enforcer, I was sent to enact punishment on the thief and recover the money. But I'm the lousy thief, the ladrón pésimo. At first, things went according to my plans."

"How much money?" Becky interrupted.

"A quarter of a million."

"Two hundred and fifty thousand dollars!" Becky gasped.

"Si," Joey responded. "It was nothing… a mere drop in the bucket to them that would make a new life for someone like me and my wife, but they will never let any thievery slide. They have been known to kill for the theft of one hundred pesos, a pittance."

"You mean you have killed for that amount," Hank hissed.

"It sounds as if there is no way out of it," Becky agreed. "They will seek justice even on one of their own."

"Especially on one of their own and his entire family," Joey added. "It is possible that they could track down Hank and Louise also… eventually."

Chapter 21

"Where is the money now?" Patrick asked.

"I have a hundred thousand in the bag, but Hank saw me before I saw him. He stole the rest."

"That's a damn lie!" Hank yelled. "I only found the money when I dumped out his bag." As he bellowed out the words, Becky jumped.

"What's wrong?" Patrick worried.

"Hank says that's a lie. That he didn't steal the money."

Joey grunted as he wondered what game Hank played now. His time was running out and he knew it. Apparently, Hank's had already run out – the little bastard was dead.

"Regardless, I'll have to arrest you for the murder of Hank Cruz," Patrick advised. "There's no way out of that for sure. You killed him in cold blood. What we don't fully understand is why you left his body at the apartment buildings. He might've lived if he hadn't been exposed to that fire and the smoke fumes."

"I didn't leave him there," Joey argued. "He ran from me. He was wounded and looking for a place to hide. He stumbled onto that place and hid so well, that I couldn't find him to finish him off. He was going to die, either way, I suppose. Lo qué sucede, sucede!"

"You're rather nonchalant about the entire thing," Becky criticized.

"Then, it is because he screwed up the plan for both of us," Joey shot back. "He hid and I couldn't get to his body. He died of smoke because he hid. Lo qué sucede, sucede!"

"What will be, will be," Patrick interpreted.

While Joey told his side of things Becky watched Hank's face grow white with shock and then livid with anger. She realized that something didn't quite add up. It was apparent that Hank didn't remember the account the same way Joey portrayed it. Becky wondered why Joey would accuse Hank of stealing a hundred and fifty thousand dollars if he didn't do it.

"Did anyone else have access to the money?" she asked.

Joey shook his head. He gazed around the motel room and then ridiculed Hank once more, "Now, that I know my stupid stepson haunts me, I have no reason to worry. You on the other hand, Miss Tibbs, are something to be feared. Hank was a weak, puny boy and now, he's an even weaker ghost, fantasma débil. I've no reason to fear him. I bet you were never a weak child. Hank is nothing like the ghouls in my Abuela's stories."

Joey started to laugh, but Hank hadn't taken his indirect threat to Becky very well. Neither had Patrick. Joey's remarks about Becky were hidden and interspersed between his assessments of his stepson, but it was still a veiled warning.

Before anyone could intervene, Hank had wrapped a thin bath towel around his stepdad's neck. Joey's chuckle became a gurgle as he gasped, and struggled to breathe. His hands clutched at the towel, trying to pry it loose, but his human strength was nothing compared to the force of an angry spirit.

Patrick moved to intervene, to attempt to release the stronghold, but Becky held up her hand to halt him as she commented, "Nothing to fear, Joey? Weak and puny? I think you should reconsider. It might be a good idea to apologize to Hank, to ask for forgiveness too. After all, you wouldn't want this angry spirit to follow you to prison, would you?"

By now, Joey's eyes bulged and his face grew fiery red. Huge streams of water ran from his eyes. He tried to say something but couldn't. "Hank, let's hear what Joey has to say," Becky calmly urged. "Can you release him for a moment?"

Her words implied that Hank was free to resume constricting Joey's breath if Joey was stubborn.

Patrick had never seen this side of Becky, not many people had, but he liked it and grinned. *"This is like good cop, bad cop,"* he silently chuckled, *"Dang! We make a great team."*

"Look, I'm sorry," Joey croaked after Hank had loosened his hold. As he rubbed his reddened throat, he continued, "I was afraid. I knew they'd come for me if I didn't find someone to blame for the crime. They'd also hold me responsible if I didn't make that person pay. I didn't have a choice. I needed someone to take the fall and I needed a body to take back with me. I'm sorry. I'm sorry that Hank picked that same time to run away. I couldn't let that opportunity pass."

"That's your apology?" Becky gasped.

"It's about as good as it gets coming from him," Hank admitted.

"Are you all right with that, Hank?" She asked next.

"I guess so. I mean, at least he said he was sorry and his excuse for stealing was to give my mother a better life. I get the sense that he came after me because I left. What I mean is that, if I'd stayed in Pueblo, he would've gone after someone else. I set myself up for that."

With that final admission, Hank was gone.

81

In an attempt to salvage at least some of the evening with Becky, Patrick called for backup. While they waited for a squad car to arrive, he read Joey his rights and handcuffed him. "Joey Ramírez, I arrest you for the murder of your stepson, Hank Cruz. In regards to the money, the cartel will have to look after their own interests. So far, nothing has been reported as stolen. Where's the weapon you used to shoot Hank?"

"It's in the nightstand drawer," Hank grudgingly answered.

Backup arrived shortly and Joey was taken away. The room was searched and the money was taken as evidence in the crime against Hank Cruz.

Jacob said, "With Hank disappearing again, I guess we have to deal with the rest of this tomorrow."

"I guess so," Becky agreed. Dreading to talk to Lou-Lou after the previous scene, Becky knew she'd have to place a call with a promise to bring Hank over on the next day.

Now, that Joey was arrested, Lou-Lou was all right with that. After she ended the call, Becky looked at Patrick and smiled, "Heck of a night, right?"

"Let's get out of here," Patrick coaxed as he put his arm around Becky's waist and pulled her close. They both shivered slightly as the familiar charge coursed through their bodies. "This has made me hungry. Want to stop and get a pint and a bite to eat?"

"What? My pasta meal from the deli didn't fill you up?" she grinned.

"It was great, but all this," he waved his arm around to indicate the motel and crew of officers going through its contents, "not to mention the ghost business, just made me really, really hungry."

"Sounds good to me," Becky agreed.

A Medium's Christmas Gift

When they entered the cozy, historic building on Haywood Road in West Asheville, Becky was pleasantly surprised. Jargon's was a warm and friendly place with vintage-inspired art and décor. Patrick ordered Trout Court bouillon, a lovely selection of fresh trout smothered in spicy tomato roux, fumet, lemon, and fennel, served over a bed of rice. Becky had several vegetarian dishes to choose from, but in the end, she ordered the Butternut Squash Agnolotti, a house-made pasta dish with butternut squash, pinyons, sage brown butter, and pecorino.

So much had happened earlier that neither Patrick nor Becky had much to say. They ate the delicious, savory meals in silence.

Many eyes, including a curious bartender named Jake, simply stared at them as the couple enjoyed the quiet, the ambiance, and each other's company.

Chapter 22

Joyce, anxious to be included in Becky's life again, arrived much earlier than she was expected the next day. But, Becky put her mother off until she was able to rouse Barbara from her drug-induced coma. Then, she returned to the kitchen to make a large pot of coffee.

Barbara stumbled into the kitchen wearing footed, onesie pajamas. Becky handed her a cup of hot coffee that she immediately slurped while her mother busily and noisily fussed over her.

"Now, honey, you can't let this get you down. You have a very bright future ahead of you. You'll see. Just try to be patient as your life unfolds. I see only great things on the horizon for you."

"Mom, please," Barb complained. "Can't I at least wake up a little before you start in?"

Joyce ignored her daughter's pleas for peace and quiet and continued to prattle until the doorbell rang. Then, she glared accusingly at Becky, "Who is that at this hour? Don't tell me you invited that young detective here! You know it was supposed to be family only!"

"He has a name, Mother. He's Patrick Burns and I would tell him anyway. He might as well be here to hear the entire conversation," Becky muttered. "Besides, he'll have comments and questions. He can ask me and then I can ask you. It'll be OK."

A Medium's Christmas Gift

Joyce shook her head in disbelief, but she didn't want to offend Becky again. The last spat had lasted well over three weeks and Joyce had just gotten back into Becky's good graces. Since it would soon be Christmas and Joyce didn't want additional conflict during that season, she held her tongue. She loved her family too much to get shut out during the happiest time of the year.

Bobby and Patrick were at the door and, although Bobby had a key, he didn't think it would be right to come in and leave Patrick on the doorstep. Becky waved them both inside and Bobby had the good sense to go on into the kitchen while Patrick gave Becky a morning kiss.

As soon as their lips met thrilling tremors coursed through each of them and they staggered closer together. "This was a mistake," Patrick whispered against Becky's cheek. "We should reserve kisses for the end of the day. How am I going to get through the morning and afternoon, feeling this way?"

Becky giggled, "Same here. We'll just have to muddle through I suppose."

"Will you go to dinner with me tonight?"

"Again?" she teased before adding, "of course."

"Pick you up at eight?"

"You bet!"

She smiled again just as Joyce impatiently called out, "Becky? Are you coming or what?"

Chapter 23

Barbara still sat at the breakfast bar drinking coffee while Joyce resumed her well-meaning barrage. Bobby saw the tension his mother caused even though she appeared to be oblivious. Having mercy on his sister, he finally tried his best to put a stop to it.

"Mom, please. Just let Barb have some coffee before you give so much support and advice."

While Bobby tried to intervene, Becky and Patrick came in to join the others. When Barb noticed Patrick, she looked alarmed and said, "Oh, I'm sorry. I'm still in my PJs. Do I need to get dressed, Becky?"

"Not in the least," Becky replied.

Joyce didn't seem to notice the conversation between her two daughters as she petted and fussed over Barbara. It wasn't until Bobby loudly cleared his throat that she looked up in surprise.

"We're all here now so could you stop bothering Barb and give us the details on Marty Smith?" Bobby asked as Becky poured cups of coffee for him and Patrick. "Why were you so convinced that it was good that Marty broke up with Barbara?"

Everyone settled down, preparing to listen.

Bobby sat beside Barb at the bar while Becky slid up on the counter near the dishwasher. Patrick stood by her side, leaning against the same counter. Joyce finally sat down beside Bobby.

"All right," Joyce began, "but none of this leaves this house!" She waited until each one nodded agreement and then continued. "Marty's father got sick when he was a senior. He didn't follow Barb to Raleigh because of that. The Smith family said he had cancer, some kind that drags on and on."

"I can't believe I got up at the butt-crack of dawn to hear something I already knew. Please, tell us something we don't know," Bobby moaned.

"Now you listen, young man," Joyce screeched. "I've had about enough of your lip. Either you apologize right this instant or I'm leaving."

At Joyce's loud ghostly racket, Barb and Becky covered their ears. Bobby made a grimace that reflected his pain also.

"Bobby!" Barbara and Becky exclaimed in unison.

"Do something before she ruptures our eardrums!" Barb cried out.

"All right, all right," Bobby said in a much nicer and more genuine voice. "I'm sorry Mom, but can't you see that all the fussing and attention you're slathering on Barb isn't helping? Please, let her breathe. And, can you please continue with your story?"

"I'm only trying to be supportive," Joyce defended, "but you have to be patient. I'm going to tell this in my own way."

"OK, Mom. Go on, please," Barb pleaded.

"It was a lie. He didn't have cancer at all. He had a mental condition, schizophrenia to be exact. The Smiths tried to hide him away. They didn't want anyone to see his severe emotional instability. Now, Marty has a similar condition."

Finally awake, Barb asked, "Are you suggesting that mental illness runs in families?"

"You shouldn't be surprised at that," Joyce said. "It seems that a lot of things run in families. Look at ours. It's not a coincidence that all of you are mediums. But I'm not a doctor," Joyce slyly countered. "It's my belief that it does. What is your professional opinion on that?"

"This is some serious accusation, Mom," Bobby cautioned, ignoring his mother's dig at Barb.

"We need a small break so I can let Patrick know what we've discovered," Becky announced. Then, she leaned in closer to Patrick and whispered, "I'm only going to give you a summary of what Mother had to say."

"Just the facts, ma'am, just the facts," Patrick softly chuckled. Then, he listened as Becky repeated the things he hadn't heard Joyce say. Everyone else silently considered the seriousness of Joyce's revelation.

Chapter 24

While Becky quietly relayed the conversation to her boyfriend, Bobby considered his mother's remark to Barb. It had hit too close to home. He knew that neither of his parents was happy that his sister's education had dragged on for so long. He also knew that it wouldn't have taken Barb nearly as much time if she didn't use her ability as an excuse. She had always been a gifted student in almost any subject and was, in fact, valedictorian of her class. If she didn't take medication to block ghosts from her life, she would've already completed her doctorate.

Obstructing her ability as a medium also hindered her cognitive aptitude for her stressful courses, but Bobby couldn't criticize his sister. If he did, he'd be the pot calling the kettle black. He knew he did the same thing by getting inebriated every blasted weekend.

At one time, he'd also had the desire to finish his education in engineering, but he was often so hammered; he couldn't get off his ass or the couch to find any kind of work except in the construction field. Bobby pushed his own drama aside for the moment and continued, "If what you say is true, it could affect Marty's life and career."

"Look," Joyce began again when Becky finished updating Patrick, "Marty was diagnosed with bipolar disorder when he was twenty-six, but his manic depression had a double aspect that included borderline personality disorder. I suspect they didn't fully understand his true condition in the beginning. Something about him having those extra features makes it more difficult to treat him. Now, his condition has worsened." Joyce paused and looked at everyone. "Does anyone have any questions about that?"

Once again, Becky repeated what Joyce had said for Patrick's benefit while the others listened to her or reflected on their own ideas and concerns. When she was finished, the conversation moved forward again.

"But how does that affect him?" Bobby asked, "I haven't noticed any real changes in him and I've known him as long as anyone."

"He would feel worried that someone he cared about would abandon him or not love him," Barbara sadly admitted. She was now clearheaded and could put all of the new information in its proper order today. "He'd also suffer intense emotions that quickly change from happy to sad. He wouldn't have a strong sense of self and would rely on the opinions of others, like his fellow officers. He would easily get very angry and not be able to control it. He'd act out that rage without censor. These symptoms describe all the recent behaviors we discussed last night."

"It does sound familiar," Bobby agreed.

"How does your sister know all this?" Patrick whispered.

"Clinical Psychology is her major and soon to be her profession once she completes her doctorate," Becky murmured.

"It's disturbingly sad," Barb commented. "I sure played my part. My abandonment, especially after Becky was kidnapped, surely pushed him over the edge. And by 'edge' I mean it caused his bizarre actions at work. He is trying to regain some form of control over his emotions after what happened between us and he took it out on Patrick and Hillary. I don't know if I can ever forgive myself for not seeing the signs earlier. It's what I know, and yet, I was so wrapped up in my own drama that this slipped past me."

Joyce immediately defended her daughter. "You're not a mind reader... How could you know? He hid this from you the same as you hid your ability from him."

"He took it out on everyone," Patrick advised, unaware that Joyce was also talking.

"What do you mean your 'abandonment' of him?" Bobby asked. "How did you ever abandon Marty Smith? You've never even dated anyone else. You've always been faithful and committed to him and your relationship."

"I can understand that you would see it that way, Bobby. But this all started the night Mom and Dad died." Barbara explained. "I knew right then that Marty would never accept this about me. I knew him too well. So, I never told him."

"That's not abandonment, Barb," Bobby argued. "That's keeping a secret at best, lying at worst."

"What you don't know is that I automatically became elusive, almost secretive, with Marty. I avoided him a lot of the time. I made excuses for not seeing him as often as we had seen each other before Mom and Dad died. I put him off at every turn. Where we once spent every weekend together, I made sure that we only saw each other when I came home which was maybe once a month. If that wouldn't cause someone to feel abandoned, I don't know what would."

"Why did you do that?" Patrick asked.

"I was afraid that if I spent more time with him, he would eventually figure out what I was hiding," Barbara sobbed.

"It's not your fault, honey," Joyce encouraged. "You didn't make Marty Smith ill. It is his destiny to battle this disorder." Fortunately, she didn't add that it was Barbara's destiny to struggle with her own vocation and purpose.

When Bobby spoke again, their attention was drawn back to the larger conversation as his voice commanded the room. "Listen, I heard everything that Barbara had to say too. Marty has bouts of depression and then bizarre spells of aggression and rage. It's an up and down, back and forth kind of disorder. I get it. I once dated a girl with a similar condition. However, here's my real concern: If this is all true, and I have no real reason to doubt it, Marty might not be able to keep his job if this gets out. It might even be dangerous for him to carry a weapon."

"That would be a tragedy, not only for him, but for his mother," Joyce thoughtfully added. "She's had to care for her husband's well-being for years. The possibility that her son is following suit is almost too much to imagine. Mr. Smith hasn't held a job in years. To be honest, she's going out of her mind with worry. If Marty lost his job, it would be an even greater financial burden to their family."

Becky repeated her mother's comments and then Patrick offered his assurances, "Let's hope it doesn't come to that. I can keep an eye on Marty. We work the same hours and shifts. I won't let him do anything foolish under my watch. And, if I see his condition escalating, if he becomes dangerous, I'll advise the Chief." He smiled at Becky and added, "Speaking of work, I have to go right now. I'll see you tonight."

"I'll walk you to the door."

Once they were in the foyer, he asked "One more kiss for the road?"

"One more kiss to carry us through the day," Becky breathlessly replied.

Chapter 25

After Patrick left, the three Tibbs siblings continued to drink coffee and discuss the situation, but their state of mind was stifled by their ever-present ghost mother. Joyce still flitted around Barbara like an annoying gnat. Her children knew she meant well but that didn't actually make her actions any less irritating.

Bobby often took charge when it came to his sisters' safety or happiness and he finally asked, "Mom, could you give us some alone time, please?"

Joyce was offended at first, but she recalled her daughters' reaction to her earlier screech and squashed an angry outburst. She also reminded herself that it was almost Christmas. Besides, Bobby had asked nicely and used a respectful tone. Joyce decided to keep her response short and sweet. However, before she could reply, Justin Tibbs appeared.

"Come on, Joyce, you simply can't seem to take a hint and as usual you've overstayed your welcome," Justin admonished.

"All right, I'm leaving. I have things to do too. I'll see all of you later," she promised.

Justin apologetically looked at his children and then quickly followed his wife. After their parents were gone, Becky curiously looked at her brother, "What did you wish to say that you couldn't say in front of Mother?"

"Probably a lot," Barb quipped.

Bobby closely looked at his older sister before he answered, "Barb's right. I have a lot to say. I wanted to remind you that you no longer have any reason to keep yourself drugged out of your mind, Barb." His blue eyes penetrated hers, probing into her deepest fears. "Now, that Marty knows and the situation is resolved, you can get back to your life. You can finish your education and start a real life with a job and security."

"Why on earth would you say that?" Barb exploded. "Nothing is resolved. Now, there is even more trouble on the horizon since Marty is acting out because of me."

"Barb, you can't let the outcome of your break up become another excuse. I'm going to tell you firsthand what I see. And, I get that you won't like it or want to hear it but, with Becky as my witness, I'm going to say it anyway."

"Well then get it off your chest," Barb gritted out, feeling more angry and insecure than sad now. She didn't like her life put under the family microscope.

"I think you've used your ability as an excuse. You've let it ruin your life when you could've had a damn fine future by now. I know that with certainty because I did the same thing."

"Bobby, you only think you know what I'm going through," Barb cut in.

"Hear me out," Bobby admonished. "Just be silent and hear what I have to say." Barb gave a curt nod so he continued. "You use drugs to block out spirits but it needs to stop."

"You're one to talk!" Barb spitefully barked. "You use alcohol to do the same thing!"

"Like I said," Bobby replied as he took a deep, deep breath. "The point I'm trying to make… what we both need to remember is that blocking our ability is unnecessary. It damages us and hurts us more than it helps us. My drinking is beginning to damage my liver. I'm sure the medications you take aren't good for you either. It has to have some serious negative physical side-effects besides making you mentally foggy."

Barb considered what Bobby had pointed out. She hated to admit that it was true. Her stomach was a mess and her general practitioner had recently told her that she was developing Irritable Bowel Syndrome (IBS). She'd recently had to add more medications to her regiment to counteract those secondary effects. She also reflected on her dopey state of mind. Would she have been aware of Marty's symptoms sooner if she hadn't tried to mask her own?

"And just what do you propose," Barb heatedly argued. "How am I supposed to deal with something on a daily basis that I despise?"

"We can set stricter ground rules for ghosts just like we did with Mom and Dad. If we did that, they would leave us alone so we could get on with our futures. I had larger plans and aspirations for my life too. Not that there's a thing in the world wrong with the job I have, but I wanted more than being a construction worker. And it wasn't my life's goal to join the military and return to Asheville as the town drunk either. I had hoped for something more, but like all of us, that changed the night our folks died. I really thought I could outrun it. I couldn't and neither can you. Surely you don't want to be a student for the rest of your life."

"Like setting boundaries and ground rules has done a lot of good," Barb groaned. "It's barely made a dent in the way mother constantly uses any excuse to hover over me."

Chapter 26

"Barbara, I happen to agree with Bobby. Please, hear him out," Becky coaxed.

"You don't get a say in this, Miss-My-Best-Friends-Are-Ghosts!" Barb turned her hostility toward her younger sister. "You've always been fine with being a medium while neither of us has been so cozy with the idea or the responsibility."

"Hold on Barb, don't be mean to Becky just because your life is in the crapper."

"Maybe you have a point, Sis," Becky asserted even though she was grateful for Bobby's defense, "but I have something valuable to add and I'd like for you to listen to me."

"Fine!" Barb stormed.

"Just think about it – Wouldn't it be nice if you were in a position to help people who see and hear things that no one else sees and hears? Wouldn't your ability as a medium give you a different take or perspective on people who exhibit those symptoms? Can't you see that your experiences could really make a difference in the way they are perceived and the way they have been conditioned to view themselves?"

"My point exactly! This isn't Salem! And our little sister has done a lot to improve public opinion about our abilities," Bobby exclaimed. "When did you get so damn smart, little Sis?"

"Look," Becky continued, ignoring Bobby's teasing remark, "I know that neither of you wanted to be mediums. You've both made it very obvious. You've each rearranged your lives and twisted yourself into knots trying to avoid it. However, despite all the things you've done, it hasn't really worked. It's my belief that you honestly don't know what you're missing until you give it a day in court."

"I don't have to try it, Becky, to know I won't like it," Barb defended.

"You don't know that. You've never helped the first ghost. Neither have you, Bobby. If you put as much effort into helping one of them as you do in avoiding them, then maybe you wouldn't see this gift as a curse. Just maybe you'd see it as rewarding and a blessing."

"What are you suggesting?" Bobby calmly asked. Becky had struck a chord within him that tingled with hope and possibilities. He knew he was ready for a change, but he wasn't sure how to go about it.

"I recommend that both of you help one ghost – just one. Assist one recently departed spirit in finding closure. Make it a point to do whatever it takes to bring about a happy ending for a ghost and their loved ones. Become comfortable with it. But, also set up strict boundaries. That works with other ghosts even though it doesn't work well with our parents. Mom gets away with abusing our rules because she knows we love her. I hate to admit it, but she takes advantage of that love. A new ghost will respect and abide by your rules. You'll see."

"Suppose that what you've said is valid," Bobby allowed, "and then, imagine that I agreed to help one ghost just to see how it feels… what's next?"

"Are you seriously considering this," Barb asked, but Bobby and Becky ignored her interruption.

"I can only imagine that you wouldn't have to drink so much," Becky alleged. "If you weren't drinking so much then you'd feel better all over in your body, mind, and soul.

I can only imagine that any type of liver problems you've noticed would naturally take care of themselves as you decrease the amount of alcohol you consume. If you were feeling better, you could probably go back to school. You know that you still have a college fund and maybe even the G.I. bill to help with those expenses. Basically, your life would change for the better. You'd probably even realize those dreams of becoming an engineer."

"And you think all this would come about from me helping just one ghost," Bobby softly grumbled.

"You asked my opinion and that's it in a nutshell," Becky declared.

"How would I go about finding one ghost to help?" Bobby thoughtfully inquired.

"Well, if it were me, I would call on someone like Jacob, set a few ground rules, and let him know I was willing to help a new ghost find closure."

"What specific ground rules would you suggest?"

"You could select one day of the week that you are willing to help. Perhaps Saturday would be an option since you have the day off. And, knowing that you are going to help a ghost that day might keep you sober on Friday night. It's tough to deal with any other problems when you have a hangover. You'll figure it out, Bobby. I know you will. On that note, I have to get to work."

Becky hadn't pointed out the obvious to her sister. She knew that Barb would apply the things she'd said to Bobby to her own situation. Barb had always been very adept at making connections. At least she was good at it when she was clearheaded and unmedicated. She'd see reason on her own.

Chapter 27

Jacob briskly paced behind the register when Becky got to work that morning. He could only surmise that, if it wasn't a ghost crisis, then it had to be a family emergency that often caused Becky to open the shop much later than she'd planned.

He knew it wasn't necessary to remind her that they needed to return to Lou-Lou's apartment to help Hank say goodbye to his sister, but he wondered how she'd squeeze that task into her packed schedule. Thankfully, he didn't have to say anything or add any more pressure on her. She cheerfully announced, "I plan to take a long lunch today so we can see Lou-Lou."

No sooner than she'd finished reassuring Jacob, the front door bells tinkled softly to indicate the first customer of the day had come in. Becky sighed and then turned to greet the young woman.

"Good morning," Becky called out in a clear voice.

"Hello, Becky. Do you have a moment to talk with me?" the petite brunette hopefully asked. However, when she noticed the confusion on Becky's face, she added, "Oh, I see you don't remember me. My name is Jennifer Toller. My mother was friends with yours. We moved away for a couple of years when I was still very young, but we returned several years ago. I believe it was shortly after your parents died. Belated condolences."

"Thank you. I do remember now," Becky smiled brightly as she pictured Jennifer as a much younger girl named Jenny. "Your mother's name is Pauline. I think most of her friends referred to her as Paulie. I know my mother did." The memory brought Paulie's face into focus too. She was an attractive brunette, much like her daughter.

"That's right," Jennifer acknowledged. "And, most everyone called me Jenny back then even though I always preferred to be called Jennifer."

"I'll keep that in mind," Becky replied before asking, "Are you looking for anything in particular?"

"No, not really. This is more of a personal nature," Jennifer confided, keeping her voice low.

"Then, how can I help?"

"My mom remarried a widower right after we returned to Asheville. In fact, that's why we came back. Mom and Jerry fell in love through the mail and while talking on the telephone. Someone our age might get to know each other in chatrooms or through texts, but they did it the old fashion way... They wrote long, romantic letters to each other and talked on the phone every day. I have to admit that they've been very happy and good for each other. To get to the point, however, just a few months ago Jerry fell ill. Now, every time my mother goes to give him his medicine, she can't find it. It's been moved or missing or turns up somewhere else in the house."

"In what way do you think I can help?"

"Becky, if the things I've heard about you are true, then you are the only one who can help." She hesitated for a brief moment and then looked around the store to make certain she wasn't overheard. "Well, it has to be a ghost, right?"

"I suppose it could be, but it could also be someone else who has access to the house. Such as a visitor, a family member, or a nurse. Would someone else play such a trick on your mother?"

Speaking of tricks, Becky wasn't totally convinced that Jennifer's visit was authentic. In her vast experience, ghosts didn't normally begin their haunting activity by merely moving objects around – unless of course, it meant something to them. There were usually some other, more obvious signs.

Becky Tibbs studied Jennifer closely to ascertain her sincerity. She knew that it didn't happen often, but she had been pranked herself on other occasions. Especially during the Christmas season. Did someone play a joke on her now? Was Jennifer an unwitting player in their game?

If it was a prank, it was more than likely a jealous store owner who wanted to ensure that Becky's popular antique shop closed during the busiest time of the year. Such tactics could occur in any profession, but the motive was often professional envy. Becky's author friend, Nicky had recently complained that a fellow author had written a bogus review of her book just to bring its ratings down. It was a hurtful tactic to use and a low blow when resentment of another's success overtook commonsense and decency.

Chapter 28

It wasn't a secret that Becky often put her ghost cases first. Almost everyone in the River Arts District knew that she would close the store early or take a very long lunch if she had a ghost case to solve. She even traveled out of town to help other city councils clear their ghost problem when it affected tourist and business revenues. And, as a business owner, everyone knew that the more hours the store remained open the better the income.

Although the antique business paid for the store's upkeep even during the worst of months, there was often little money left for other things. It was the money Becky made from ghost-related cases that paid those incidentals, including groceries and utilities at the family home she'd inherited.

Becky looked around her lovely store now. It was well-stocked with the most popular and trendy items with many small antique furniture pieces that made the perfect gift for loved ones. She also carried a surprising amount of vintage glassware, including Carnival, Depression, elegant, Fenton, and Milk glass. All of it was available in almost any color and style. And, although her glassware was one of her biggest sellers this time of year, she also carried an amazing collection of vintage costume jewelry that also sold well during the holiday season.

Some people thought that all the residents in Asheville were hippies, but it wasn't true. Asheville was home to a diverse collection of peoples with many different tastes and beliefs. Although it was true that many women in the area preferred hemp strung beads or hand-blown glass pendants and medallions, some desired a new-to-them rhinestone necklace to complete their festive holiday attire.

As Becky admired the merchandise, she fretted a little bit. She'd already lost several days of income by closing the store to recover from injuries suffered during her recent abduction. She didn't relish closing up again unless she had to do so. She needed her store's sales as much as the next person did, maybe more.

Her thoughts returned to Jennifer as she continued, "This has been going on for weeks now and Mom is at her wit's end. Do you think you could stop by and help us?"

Remember, my dear child, you also have a life and shouldn't allow others to interrupt the plans you've made with those you love, Zetmeh advised referring to her date with Patrick that night.

"What else has your mom noticed, Jennifer?"

"Mom says the lights flicker on and off in Jerry's room. Sometimes, she goes to sit with him to read a book out loud. They both love cozy mysteries. The lights crackle and pop before they go off. It scares her because this seems to only happen in his room when she sits with him. She knows the wiring is good. Jerry was an electrician and he made sure all the wiring was up to code. I don't know what else I can tell you. I looked it up on the internet and from what I've read, it could be a ghost."

"Has anyone died recently?" Becky asked.

"No, not recently. Both my dad and Jerry's wife died about ten years ago."

"I can stop by your home on Monday after I close for the evening," Becky offered. "Will that work for you and Paulie?"

"Yes, thank you, but you do realize that's Christmas Eve, right?" Jennifer gushed.

"I admit that I didn't," Becky replied. "I guess the date slipped up on me. However, I'm almost certain that it won't take long to solve your problem."

"Thank you so much," Jennifer said as she hurriedly scribbled down the address and her phone number. Next, she handed Becky a check in the standard amount before she left.

More customers came in, but other than Jennifer, no one else had a ghost problem to discuss. Becky had a very busy and productive morning as Asheville citizens prepared for the Christmas season. At noon, Becky put a sign on the door that read, "Be Back as Soon as I Can."

Chapter 29

When she arrived at Lou-Lou's little cottage, Jacob and Hank were already there waiting for her. Becky was relieved to see that Hank's sister was calm and collected which allowed them to get down to business.

"Lou-Lou, Hank is here," Becky began.

"Oh, Hank," Louise gushed, "thank you so much for making it possible for me to live here. I'm just so sorry that you won't be here too. I'm so sorry that I told Joey where you were. I know it's my fault that he shot and killed you. I'm so very sorry about that and I hope you can forgive me. I was looking forward to our new life here and I'm very sorry that it didn't work out that way. I'll miss you."

"Lou-Lou, it's all right," Hank replied through Becky. "I don't want you to be sad or have regrets. The way I look at it is that everything happened the way it was supposed to happen. I'm just glad you are safe now."

"Hank, is there anything else I can do for you?' Becky asked after she'd given Louise his message.

"Just tell Lou-Lou that the car is hers. I didn't have a will, but she is my next of kin so I hope the car will transfer to her easily enough. It's very important to me that she has the car and that it's in her name. If there is any way that you can assist her with the car, I'd be very grateful."

"I'll do what I can," Becky replied. "Are you ready to crossover to the other side now?"

"Yes, but before I go, please tell Lou-Lou what I just said."

Becky repeated Hank's wishes word for word and the ghost brother carefully watched his sister's eyes for any sign of acknowledgment that she'd fully understood his hidden message. As brother and sister, they'd used the technique often in the past. By stressing key points and repeating words they'd been able to survive under Joey Ramirez's horrible parenting. Lou-Lou realized that Hank not only had a message for her but he was trying to hide something from Becky. He seemed anxious to leave before the medium could discover this. She rapidly blinked her eyes several times and Hank relaxed. Knowing that she'd understood, and with his final unfinished business now complete, he turned to Becky.

"I'm ready, Becky. I'd like to thank you and Jacob for your patience and help."

Becky called down the light and Hank crossed over without any worries or fears. He knew his sister would be safe and that was what mattered most to him.

After Hank was gone, Becky and Jacob were anxious to get back to the shop. She'd been gone for over an hour and still had so much to do. Jacob simply wanted to return to his friends, Lois and Myrtle.

Louise could barely contain her excitement as Becky prepared to leave. She waited until Becky's truck had pulled out of the driveway and was out of sight before she rushed outside to her brother's car. She knew the keyword in his final message indicated that it was more than merely a desire for her to have ownership of his car. It was coded to let her know that he'd left something more in the vehicle.

She searched the trunk, including the wheel well, but didn't find anything. She recalled that Becky's cute boyfriend was a police officer. Patrick had found the car and brought it to her... Did he recover whatever Hank had intended for her? She felt certain that if he had, it would've been mentioned before now. And since no one brought it up, she continued to search.

She examined every inch of the vehicle. She pulled back the floor mats. She looked in the glove box, in the tight space under the front seats, all the door compartments, and even pressed the overhead padding and the front and back dashboards to see if something had been hidden there.

Nothing.

She went over the car again and was just about to give up when she noticed a space beneath the rear bench seat. With a little tugging and pulling, she was able to pop the seat out of its clips to find a storage space under it.

Louise almost fainted when she saw a large pile of cash neatly tucked in each depression. "My goodness, there must be thousands of dollars here! Oh, my sweet brother, thank you so much!" She joyfully cried out.

There was also a blood-stained note that read, "Lou-Lou, if you're reading this then I'm probably dead. Joey shot me. This money is for you. Be careful with it and keep it a secret. Joey stole it, but something tells me that he's the cartel's problem now. Just use it sparingly and have a good life. Take care of yourself and know that you are a good person. You deserve a little happiness. I love you."

Chapter 30

That night after Patrick picked Becky up for their date; they went to the West Asheville Pub to have dinner. The pub was a hotspot for locals to gather and sample the various locally brewed beers. It was crowded that Saturday night with only a few remaining tables available. In this bar, folks didn't just order, eat, and go. They lingered.

While Patrick and Becky waited for a pint of cold ale to arrive, she perused the menu and then confessed, "I hope you don't think I'm fickle, Patrick, but I've noticed that my mood is sometimes erratic. I've heard that eating a strict vegetarian diet can do that to a person, especially when it's a new change. In order to balance out those effects, I've come to the conclusion that it doesn't hurt to eat meat once or twice a week. I'd like to order the Black and Blue burger unless that changes your opinion of me."

Patrick guffawed.

"What?" Becky asked unsure whether or not she should be offended.

"You!" he exclaimed. "You're adorable. You're honest and kind, sweet and well-mannered. You're also optimistic and sentimental. In my limited experience, these characteristics are missing in a lot of young women I've known. It's a rare gift and I, for one, truly appreciate this about you. How could you honestly think I'd be offended that you take care of yourself? I'll have one too. We'll be black and blue and balanced together." He chuckled again.

"Really?" Becky asked.

"Absolutely," he confirmed. "I'm all for you being healthy and happy. Besides, that burger comes slathered with veggies such as onions and tomatoes which are good for the heart. How could that be unhealthy?"

"That's true," Becky agreed.

"How was your day? Anything new with Hank and Lou-Lou?"

"They said their goodbyes and it was very touching. What about you? Did anything unusual happen at the police department today?"

"Marty behaved himself if that's what you mean. He didn't kick anything or chew anybody out. It was a relief," he admitted. However, just as he mentioned Marty, his sergeant came in with Patty Lawless. Marty and Patty strode behind Becky on their way to the only available table. "Oh, crap."

"What now?" Becky asked looking around to discover what had caused his reaction.

"Marty just came in with Patty."

"Well, that can't be good," Becky observed, but then she noticed that Bobby also came in with Hillary. They were dressed casually, but Hillary looked radiant in black leather pants and a red sweater. She wore her hair down and the wavy curls glistened with shea butter in the overhead lighting. It was most becoming.

Even though Becky knew that Hills had always had a secret crush on Bobby, their date was almost as surprising as it was to see Marty and Patty together. Becky was fine with Bobby dating Hillary – if it worked out, but she didn't want her best friend hurt if it didn't. She worried that Hills would end up only a name in a long list of other girls who had fallen for Bobby's charisma.

Bobby leaned against the edge of their table briefly and asked, "You two want to be alone or can we join you?"

"You might wish we were with you when Patty executes her next attack, Becky," Hills advised as she nodded at the couple sitting a few tables over.

"She might be right, Patrick," Becky agreed. "Every time I've been out lately, Patty makes a point to try to start something."

"Then, we better join you," Bobby concluded as he observed the crowded pub. "Otherwise we'll be standing or lucky enough to get a seat at the bar."

"Look, I don't mind you joining us, but don't assume that I can't take care of Becky," Patrick quickly asserted.

"Never entered my mind," Bobby allowed, "It's just that I'd like to see Patty's drama play out firsthand. And, I'm curious how Marty will react too."

"Heck yeah," Hills quipped, "If you let us join you, we've got a front-row seat!"

The server hurried over to take their order so that all four plates would arrive at the same time. "So, y'all are making my job easy tonight. Everyone wants the Black and Blue with fries," she confirmed, making sure she had jotted it down correctly after Bobby and Hills placed their orders.

"You have it right," Patrick replied for all of them.

Bobby and Hills looked questioningly at Becky, but she quickly reassured, "Well yeah, I'm starving for that right now."

"She wanted it the last time we were here, but she avoided the temptation with an artichoke dip. I guess your mother's advice sits better with you now." Hills added.

"Yours and hers," Becky agreed.

They still had a few minutes before their food would arrive, but meanwhile, they enjoyed the flavorful beers. The time seemed to skip ahead when Patty flounced over to their table without Marty.

She wore a short, black skirt with knee-high black boots and a little black and white bolero jacket over a bright-red sequined bustier. If Patty wasn't Patty and such a pain in the neck to everyone, they might've complimented the festive attire. But it was Patty and she was a sore spot so no one made any comments.

"Look at you slumming it, Bobby Tibbs! The big captain of the football team has fallen off his pedestal. I never dreamed that I'd see you out and about with Asheville's main outcasts and freaks!"

"You need to get out of the past, Patty, and let that high school crap go!" Hills interjected. "That time is long gone."

"Just because I've never been out with you, don't make assumptions, Patty. Now, that would truly be called lowering my standards," Bobby countered. "But, tell me, Patty, how on earth did you get a date with Marty Smith anyway?"

"He needed a shoulder to cry on after the nasty breakup with your sister," Patty cooed. She felt extremely elated to be out with Marty and she didn't let Bobby's crass remark bother her in the least. She assumed he was simply jealous anyway. Then, her face lit up as she thought of something, "Oh, that's right!" she feigned shock. "What am I thinking? You and Barbara are mutants too! This is too rich! Who would've ever thought that the high and mighty Tibbs family was chockfull of crazies and aberrations? The bible warns about keeping company with the likes of you which makes me wonder why Patrick Burns is in the midst of such heathen company."

"It also warns about morally loose women like you, you brazen hypocritical hussy!" Hillary blasted in her best southern drawl.

Becky noticed that Bobby laid a calming hand over Hillary's. It was an intimate gesture even if he'd only intended it to soothe his date.

"Is it a real date? What happened between those two after we left last night?" Becky silently wondered, but

her attention was drawn back to the conversation when she heard Patrick's mellow voice.

"Sooner or later Marty will lose interest, Patty. He'll have to get a restraining order to keep you away just like I did. With your current charges of vandalism and malicious criminal mischief, I'm sure your probation officer would be shocked to know how often you violate your conditions, I suggest you move along."

Patty's bright red pouting lips turned into a sneer as she shrilled, "Ever since you started dating this circus clown, you've become a bore anyway, Patrick Burns!"

Her piercing voice seemed to jar Marty out of a dazed stupor. When he heard Patrick's name loudly called out, he turned to look. Without saying a word, he gulped down the rest of his beer, threw a wad of bills on the table, and got up to leave. On his way out, he grabbed Patty by the arm. "What the hell do you think you're doing, Patty? It's time to go." He curtly nodded at Bobby and Patrick and ignored Becky and Hills.

"That went better than I expected," Hills joked.

"Well, the mood is ruined now," Bobby confessed as he looked at Becky. "What do you say we get our food to go and try to salvage the night at my place?"

"That sounds like a terrific idea," Hills agreed. "What do you say, Becky? Will you and Patrick join us?"

Becky looked at Patrick. She wasn't sure if he'd think it was such a great way to spend their evening. And, she didn't know if she was up for it either. It seemed like every time they tried to have a few moments alone, someone or something got in the way.

Patrick felt the same way, but he didn't want to disappoint Becky if she really wanted to join the others. He nodded and Bobby went to the bar to let the server know to pack up their food.

Chapter 31

When they got to Bobby's new house, Rings was excited to see everyone. He eagerly yapped as he bounded from Bobby to Becky, to Hills, and then to Patrick.

Naturally, neither Hillary nor Patrick could see or hear the animated, Dalmatian ghost puppy, but they could feel his soft paws pressing against their thighs as he stood on hind legs whining for them to pet him. Hills jumped back in alarm and stepped on one of the pup's toes.

The puppy let out a high-pitched yelp that caused the lights to flicker. "Oh, poor puppy," Becky soothed.

"Calm down, Rings," Bobby called out. "Here boy, come to your Aunt Becky and leave our friends alone."

Having never been to Bobby's home, Hills blurted, "Now what? You have a ghost dog... a dog that no one can see except you? You never mentioned that either, Becky. What else haven't you told me?"

"That's probably it," Bobby joked. "You know all our family secrets now. What are you going to do with them?"

Becky suddenly realized that Bobby was serious about Hillary. Even though he'd had a slew of other women over, somehow he'd managed to keep Rings a secret. Now, he'd deliberately let Hills meet his ghost puppy. As she pondered that, her heart thrilled when she considered that he'd also allowed Patrick to be part of his inner circle. She reminded herself that this was a good thing and quickly got on board.

"Here Patrick, come sit next to me on the sofa. You too, Hills. I'll introduce you to Rings," Becky encouraged.

After they were seated on either side of her, Becky took Patrick's left hand and placed it on the puppy's head. "See," she cooed. "Can't you tell he's just adorable from his soft, fluffy fur?"

Rings wiggled and squirmed under Patrick's hand and finally nibbled on his fingers. Patrick laughed.

"Me, too," Hills eagerly chirped.

Becky placed Hillary's right hand on Rings as she described the puppy to them, "Rings is a Dalmatian puppy and from the looks of him, he's about six months old. He has white fur with lots of black spots, but he deserved the name 'Rings' because he has a large black ring around each eye. He used to live in the River Arts District until Bobby brought him to live here."

"Are there many ghost dogs?" Hills asked.

"Rings is the only one I've ever seen," Becky replied.

"What about ghost cats?" Hills asked next.

"I've never seen one, but that doesn't mean they don't exist. To be quite honest, pets usually cross over right away the same as young children and babies."

"Then why didn't Rings cross over?" Patrick asked as he continued to stroke the puppy's back and ears.

"We're not sure yet," Becky said as she looked at Bobby. Her brother only shrugged his shoulders. He didn't seem to know either.

Becky knew that Rings had a purpose, but it was too delicate to discuss in front of everyone present. One day Bobby would know the reason too, especially if he stopped shirking his gift and his responsibilities to the dead.

"Let's eat!" Bobby announced. "I'm starving and we don't want the buns and fries to get soggy."

The food had been packed in individual plastic boxes. They placed the containers on their laps and began to savor the juicy burger and crispy fried potatoes.

"I have to tell you," Patrick admitted, "I don't care what anyone else says; you two are not freaks. What you do for this community is amazing. I'm just glad to be a part of it."

"Me too," Hills agreed and then added, "What do you think Marty was doing with Patty Lawless tonight?"

"I can only speak from a male's perspective, but I suspect that it was a rebound date," Bobby replied.

"I agree," Patrick admitted.

"We all know about rebounds, but why do you think that he chose Patty?" Becky innocently asked.

"Marty's heart is broken and he misses female companionship. He can't have Barbara and he's not ready to get involved with anyone else that might be a suitable replacement. Hence, he picked the worst possible option. He'll date a girl he knows he could never care about," Bobby informed. He smiled at Becky. "Sorry Sis, that's just the way it works sometimes. We men are dogs."

"Aw, come on Bobby. Don't lump all of us into that category. The best way to describe this situation is that Patty is an interim. Someone to get him through his heartache," Patrick added.

Rings yapped loudly when he heard his owner stop speaking. Bobby and Becky laughed at his antics and then shared the joke with Patrick and Hills.

"Seriously," Hills asked, "what's it like taking care of a ghost puppy? Ever slip on a wet spot or doggy doo?"

The others laughed at her questions.

"I have to admit that it's surprisingly easy," Bobby said. "Rings doesn't require any special attention. He's the best kind of pet for me. I don't have to walk him or feed him. He is forever a puppy with boundless energy. He doesn't eat so there's no poop to clean up. It's the best of all worlds because all he wants is a little love."

"Aw, that was actually sweet even if men are dogs," Hills declared. "That's why you guys are dog people."

"Come on now," Bobby rejoined, "like Patrick said, don't lump us all in that same group. We have feelings too."

Hills punched him lightly on the shoulder, "You know what I mean, Bobby Tibbs."

"I personally love cats," Becky added.

"I could abide by Rings," Hills laughed." He doesn't even smell."

"Cats are cool too," Becky defended. "They're independent and smart, sassy and playful." But it seemed that no one noticed her cat comments.

"Not to change the subject," Bobby said, "Except, I have to ask, Is Patty always that hostile to the two of you?"

"Sometimes she's worse," Hillary admitted.

"Let's just say that we avoid her when we can and try to muddle through when she catches us unaware," Becky agreed.

"Sounds fun," Bobby remarked, but his cynical tone showed that he didn't think it was the slightest bit amusing.

"Now that she's focused on Marty, maybe she won't be consumed with hating me," Becky sounded hopeful.

"Why do you say that?" Bobby asked.

"We dated for a couple of weeks," Patrick stated. "As soon as she saw me with Becky, she started throwing darts at your sister."

"How long ago did you date her?" Hills asked.

"Almost five years ago when I was very naïve."

"And, she's still hanging on?" Bobby frowned. "That's some serious stalking behavior. Do I need to worry about my little sister? I mean, has Patty ever been violent or destructive?"

"Only with inanimate objects and destruction of personal property," Patrick allowed. "Don't worry; I'll keep a close eye on things."

"Four eyes are better than two," Bobby concluded.

"All right, we'll both keep an eye on things," Patrick agreed.

"You guys make me feel like I'm a little child that might chase her ball out into the street," Becky complained.

"Becky Tibbs, you're the most innocent, sweetest person I know," Hills contended. "If these big strong men want to protect you, then just shut up and let them."

"You shut up," Becky giggled as she leaned against her best friend.

Chapter 32

"While we're all here together, what's everyone doing for Christmas?" Bobby asked. "It's next week. Has anyone made plans?"

Becky gasped. She was more than a bit shocked that her brother brought up the topic without consulting her first. She and Patrick hadn't even had a chance to discuss it.

It was presumptuous of Bobby to assume that her relationship with Patrick had reached that level. Special holidays were normally reserved for families – Only the most committed couples spent Christmas with each other. It had only been four weeks since they'd met and she wasn't completely convinced they were a serious couple – yet.

"Did I put you on the spot?" Bobby teased when he noticed Becky's cheeks turn a bright shade of pink.

"Girl, you need to drag your butt into this century," Hills teased. "It's OK to be shy and reticent, but totally unnecessary."

"I had hoped to spend Christmas with Becky," Patrick confessed as he reached to take her hand. "Is that a possibility?"

"I plan to cook Christmas dinner. I hadn't thought past that, but you are more than welcome to join us. You too Hills. Sorry, it didn't occur to me earlier. I only assumed that each of you would want to spend it with your own immediate families."

"Are you kidding?" Hills and Patrick said at the same time.

"Why not?" Bobby asked.

"Becky knows how wrecked I was when all the family came in during Thanksgiving and it only gets worse at Christmas," Hills admitted.

"Same for me," Patrick agreed. "I'd rather eat with a bunch of strangers at an all-night-diner than listen to all the backbiting that takes place in my family when they get together."

"Thanks!" Becky choked.

"Oh no!" Patrick quickly replied. "Not comparing you or your family to that at all. I'd love to spend the holiday with you."

"Well then, it's a date," Bobby eagerly concluded as he smiled at Hillary. "By the way, Becky, since you can have meat now, will our Christmas dinner be vegetarian or can I count on a turkey?"

"I suppose we can have a turkey," she agreed.

"Let me bring the meat," Patrick quickly offered. "The department hands out smoked hams and turkeys to each officer at Christmas. You won't have to do anything except warm it. Is that all right?"

"It's wonderful," Becky assured. "Thank you."

After she was home that night and ready for bed, Becky thought about Bobby. She wasn't sure what was going on with her brother. He seemed to be turning over a new leaf. It was exciting and terrifying at the same time. She loved the Bobby she knew. What if the leaf flipped back over leaving a broken heart in its wake? She knew Hillary was a big girl and she'd also done her part to warn her of the dangers in dating Bobby.

Becky recalled the conversation that she and Hills had on her patio shortly after her abduction rescue. Hills had wanted to know what she thought about the new detective who had saved her, but Becky had described her joy at seeing Bobby instead…

"I didn't even know he was there. In my woozy state, I could only see Bobby. I've never been happier to see my brother, Hills. Never!"

"Yeah, Bobby is something to behold. That's for sure," Hills admitted.

"Wait, are you hoping to catch Bobby's eye one day just like Patty Lawless suggested? Because I have to tell you, Hills, that he is not the type to stick around."

"Well, sure he is, Becky. He just hasn't found the right one. That's how it always is. They ain't until they are."

"You're sure about that, Hills? Would you risk taking a chance that you're the one, knowing full well that he'd move on if you weren't?"

Hills took a deep breath and then drawled, "I don't know if I'm hung up on Bobby or not… not really. I know I love you. I know I admire him. He's surely good eye-candy. And, to be quite honest, I haven't found anyone else worth fantasizing about. So let a girl have her little private dreams, Becks."

Now, Bobby and Hills had been on a date and seemed very happy and at ease with each other. As she remembered the phrase Patrick had translated when they were with Joey Ramírez – what will be will be - Becky sighed and rolled over to get some sleep.

She heard Zetmeh whisper,

Que será, será.

Chapter 33

Sunday morning, Bobby Tibbs woke up in his big, king-size bed all alone. In the past, Friday night through Monday morning, he'd have had some girl; any girl would do, sprawled out beside him. It was his normal routine to start drinking as soon as he got off work and only stop when it was time to head back to the job.

That habit usually included buying shots for anyone willing to spend a "Weekend at Bobby's." There were plenty of willing young women who were more than eager to do so. He'd always been popular with the ladies... and he knew it.

But, something had changed in Bobby.

Whether it was Darwinism, existentialism, or some other creative power, he couldn't say. All he knew is that a shift had occurred in him. He realized he felt different. He understood that he had a choice and a voice, even a calling if someone wanted to take it that far.

He realized he *was* different.

Since the talk with both his sisters, something had definitely changed in Bobby. He was tired of the way he'd done things in the past. He wanted something more. As he stretched his arms and legs out in all four directions, he felt good. He felt... happy. He couldn't remember the last time he'd felt that way.

Was it before his folks died?

Becky's suggestion that he help a ghost had really settled in on him. It made sense in the most peculiar way. It also rang true. He'd almost decided to move away after her disturbing case about Josh Edwards a few months back. He'd witnessed the struggles she'd endured when trying to help her long, lost boyfriend and it had disturbed him. She had put herself in danger to help a ghost. Sure, Josh was her first boyfriend, but she could've been seriously injured.

Bobby had admired Becky more at that time than ever before. She was fearless. She'd proved that once more when she was abducted only a few weeks ago.

After the case with Josh, Bobby had compared his life to Becky's; he hadn't liked what he'd seen. He'd seen that he was a selfish bastard that stayed drunk to block out all spiritual activity – even the good stuff. He'd hated himself for it. He'd wanted to change but he didn't know how.

He'd finally come to the conclusion that he needed to move away and start over. He'd made some positive plans to do that, but as time slipped by, those resolutions had slithered out of sight too. Then, he'd experienced more of the same. He'd drunk too much, been with too many women, and generally pissed away his life. He was in a rut so deep that it might as well be his own grave. The saddest part, he didn't know how to dig himself out of it… not until Becky had thrown him a lifeline just the other day.

As he considered it now, he realized that running wasn't the answer. He could run from a lot of things but he couldn't escape who he was. He quickly made up his mind to embrace his ability that very day.

Rings scrambled up on the bed and jumped on his chest before he licked his owner's face. Bobby had to admit that Rings had given him a lot of joy since he'd brought the puppy home with him a few months back. And, something else… Rings had made him feel love and loved.

A Medium's Christmas Gift

Bobby knew that, if he wanted to take a day to help a ghost, he was already off to a good start. It was Sunday and he was sober without a hangover. "A new experience," he chuckled as he rubbed Rings vigorously across his back and head.

It was still early, so Bobby got dressed and headed downtown. If any ghost needed help, that's where they'd be... hanging out near Mission Hospital. It seemed that Jacob had the River Arts District well-covered and seldom ventured into the downtown area unless he'd heard of a problem.

With a destination in mind, Bobby first stopped at Penny Cup Coffee. He ordered the coffee and bagel to go and ate the warm bread while finding a parking spot.

One ghost, in particular, caught his eye. She was older, but something about her reminded him of Barbara, She was tall and thin and had a distinctive vibe that muted her good looks. He knew that, like his sister, this woman wanted her work or career to be taken seriously and wouldn't allow her good looks to get in the way of that ambition.

She wasn't a part of the crowd that clustered around the hospital, she was on the sidewalk. She wore flannel pajamas and an open terrycloth robe. The belt to the robe trailed behind her. She looked out of place, to say the least.

When she saw Bobby looking directly at her, she asked, "Wait, can you see me?"

"I can see you," he replied. When the other ghosts saw his exchange with her, they rushed to him, but Bobby held up his hand, "Not today people. I'll come back another time. Today I'll help her first."

He was pleased to see that they backed away. Becky had been right. Setting boundaries did work with everyone except their mother. He liked that immediately and turned back to look questioningly at the ghost he intended to help.

"Duh, you want to know why I'm still here?" she asked.

"Something is keeping you here," Bobby agreed. "Do you have a name and do you want to tell me about your unfinished business?"

"I'm Sue Ellen Croft and I lost my cat."

Bobby chuckled in spite of himself. "I'm Bobby."

"I know who you are."

"You do?" he asked in surprise.

"Yeah, ghost radar or something like that, but I thought that you didn't help ghosts."

"Today's your lucky day," Bobby grinned. "Now, where did you last see your cat?"

He wondered if he'd have to call the fire department to get her lost feline off the roof or out of a tree, but he was set on helping her.

"That's just it," Sue Ellen explained, "It was so cold and we'd cuddled up together in my bed. The next thing I remember was people in my apartment. They said I was dead and that my kitten was dead too. Carbon monoxide poisoning took us in our sleep. I didn't have the right kind of smoke detectors. That's all I know except that this sucks to go out because of the wrong equipment."

Bobby recalled Becky's statement about young children and pets crossing over immediately, he took that on faith and explained, "I believe that if you can't find your cat that indicates he has already crossed over."

"She," Sue Ellen corrected. "My kitten was a she."

"All right, but she has already gone to the other side," he patiently affirmed.

"I saw her after I was dead. She was still in the apartment, and then she got out the window that they left open. They were trying to air out the rooms so the coroner could come in."

"Wait," Bobby interrupted, "are you saying that you saw your kitten after you were both dead?"

"That's exactly what I'm saying. She was a ghost too and I can't leave until I find her."

"I'm not sure that's how it works," Bobby advised. "In fact, I'm pretty sure it's not how it works."

"What do you mean?"

"Well, believe it or not, dogs and cats and all other pets have unfinished business too. If they aren't finished, they don't leave."

"Will you please come back to my apartment and look for her anyway?" Sue Ellen begged.

"Lead the way."

The apartment wasn't far, just a few blocks up the street and then another block to the east. Bobby walked beside Sue Ellen in silence as she led him there. Police tape covered the entrance door, but Bobby slipped under it and entered the cozy studio that was still being "aired out."

"Where did you say you last saw your cat?"

"She was playing around and under the bed, but all the people coming and going scared her. She went out this window as soon as they opened it." Sue Ellen pointed to one in a row of three identical windows that were all still open.

Bobby stuck his head out the opening and looked around. He didn't see a cat but he still called out, "Here, kitty kitty. Here, kitty kitty."

They both heard a soft meow coming from the above ledge. Bobby turned and looked up to see the cutest little white Persian kitty with a delicate pink nose and pink tipped ears. She wore a pink ribbon around her neck and it had caught on a piece of wrought iron railing.

"I've got you, little kitty, I've got you," Bobby coaxed, but she struggled to avoid his grasp. "What's her name?" he called out to Sue Ellen.

"Prissy," Sue Ellen replied. "Because she looks like a little princess. Keep your voice soft and soothing and she'll come to you."

"Her ribbon is caught on the railing. She thinks she's trapped and can't come to me," Bobby explained.

"Are you saying she isn't actually trapped?"

"The way I understand it, a ghost, even an animal ghost, can think of a place and they simply blink to that location," Bobby inadvertently gave Sue Ellen her first ghost lesson.

"How do you know this? I mean, I'm the first ghost you've ever helped... so how would you know that?"

"I guess all the things I've heard my sister say about ghosts and their abilities must've stuck with me."

Sue Ellen considered his advice for a moment and then thought of her trapped kitten. In an instant, she was there on the ledge beside Prissy. She delicately picked up the kitten and hugged her tightly as she soothed, "Oh my pretty, pretty kitty. I thought I'd lost you." Then, in the next instant, they were back inside the apartment.

Bobby looked at Sue Ellen while she petted and stroked Prissy. They were reunited and happy so his work was done. Wasn't it? He hated to interrupt the reunion but he also wanted to complete his mission to help one ghost. He wondered if Becky would give him bonus points for helping two ghosts even if it was a kitten. He cleared his throat, "Um, Sue Ellen, are you ready to cross over now?"

"I'm as ready as I'll ever be."

"Did you need for me to tell anyone anything else?"

"Nope, I don't feel as if I've left anything undone. I'm ready," she repeated.

Bobby had hoped that she needed something else. This had seemed too easy and he wasn't sure what to do next. He'd seen Becky bring down the light to open a doorway to the other side – she'd done it for Josh, but he didn't have a clue about how to do it. Bobby didn't often feel insecure or hesitant, but he certainly felt that way now.

Vowing he'd be sure to ask Becky more questions, he didn't have long to consider it. It seemed like only a few moments had passed when Sue Ellen's mother and aunt came to meet her. They stood on either side of her and each clasped her arm in theirs as they welcomed her. As she prepared to leave with them, she thanked Bobby for helping her, but he could tell she was actually giddy to be going.

The three women moved toward a doorway made of some kind of gelatinous light. Bobby couldn't believe what he was seeing. If the jelly-like matter had been encased in a ring, it would've looked exactly like a stargate from *SG1*, a television series he used to watch. He was stunned that the reality of what he witnessed was so similar to the likeness of fiction.

Sue Ellen glanced back at him for a brief moment before they completely disappeared. That's when he got another huge shock. Prissy made a flying leap back into Bobby's earthly plane and directly into his arms.

Sue Ellen's mouth formed a perfect 'O' and then she was gone. There wasn't anything either of them could do. Prissy purred a low thrumming sound and arched her back as she rubbed against his chest and her feet made a kneading motion on his arm.

"Well, Prissy how about that," Bobby murmured in response. "I guess you weren't through after all. We'll have to see what Rings has to say about you. Yes, we will."

Chapter 34

Monday, was the most profitable day Becky had experienced so far during the Christmas spree. The bells on the store's front door played a constant melody as shoppers hurried in for last-minute gifts. Becky didn't even have a spare minute for lunch. By closing time, she was exhausted but pleased with the boom in business.

That evening while Becky drove to the address Jennifer had given her, she mentally prepared herself to help Paulie with her ghost problem. Meanwhile, Patrick arrived at Bobby's home. Becky's brother had called to encourage him to drop by and, even though he didn't know the reason for the impromptu invitation, Patrick went. He thought too much of Becky to disappoint Bobby.

While Bobby waved Patrick inside, Jennifer greeted Becky at the front entrance of her mother's home.

"Thank you for coming Becky, especially on Christmas Eve. Follow me, please. Mother will be excited that you are here."

Jennifer led Becky into the living room of the small but gracious, three-bedroom home that Paulie shared with her husband, Jerry. Paulie was seated near the fireplace and busily worked to crochet a granny-stitch afghan. Time had turned her once brunette tresses into a pretty platinum blonde.

Paulie looked up when they entered and greeted Becky with a sweet smile. "I'm trying to finish a last-minute Christmas gift, she explained as she set aside her needle and thread. "Hello, Becky. My goodness, Jennifer doesn't have to introduce you. You look so much like your mother I'd know you anywhere. I was very sorry to hear of your parents' deaths."

"Thank you," Becky smiled a response. "Jennifer has told me about your problem. How can I help?"

"We all want this resolved as quickly as possible, I know. I'm sure you want to get home to your family. Come with me," Paulie indicated as she stood up. "You'll see."

Paulie led Becky to her husband's bedroom and as they entered the room the lights began to flicker erratically. It wasn't necessary for Becky's benefit. She could see the dark-haired woman who lingered by Jerry's bedside.

"Well finally!" the middle-aged ghost replied. "I've been trying to get someone's attention for ages."

"What is your name and how can I help you?" Becky asked.

"My name is Mary Beth and I'm Jerry's first wife."

"So why are you haunting this room?"

"Because she keeps giving him medicine that could kill him!" Mary Beth screeched. Her loud reaction caused the lights to blink off and on and Paulie felt an icy draft in the air. She briskly rubbed her arms to dispel the chill and then moved closer to Jerry to adjust his covers.

Jerry was sleeping, but other than being in bed, he appeared to be healthy. He didn't seem to be dehydrated or undernourished. His complexion was pink and even-toned. Becky began to wonder what was keeping Jerry in bed.

"What do the doctors say is wrong with Jerry?" Becky quietly asked, directing the question to Paulie.

"He's depressed," Mary Beth cried out as the lamp on the bedside table went out. It sputtered to life again and Becky continued to question Paulie.

"Paulie when did Jerry fall ill?"

"I suppose it was a couple of months ago. I didn't notice at first. We've been very happy and active in our retirement. We like to go out to antique shows and flea markets on occasion. You know, take little day trips... we often went downtown to have lunch but suddenly, Jerry just didn't feel like going anymore. He felt too tired."

"And when did you notice the lights flickering and the medicine disappearing?"

"It was about a month later, shortly after his doctor changed his medicine."

"See?" Mary Beth shouted. "The doctor changed his medicine and what he's giving him could kill Jerry!"

"Hold on, Paulie," Becky cautioned. "Mary Beth is here and she seems to think that the new medication could cause serious harm to Jerry. Let me ask her a few questions so we can sort this out."

"Mary Beth, his first wife?" Paulie exclaimed in alarm. "Why would she be here? Is Jerry dying?"

"Let me try to find out why she's here," Becky calmly replied.

"Mary Beth, why did you say that?"

"Jerry went to the doctor because he has anxiety attacks and depression. He didn't want to admit it to her, but he's always had them. I guess he thought she wouldn't understand. When he has an attack, it becomes difficult for him to breathe. The doctor on call misread his symptoms and prescribed a bronchodilator, but Jerry also has a mild heart condition that hasn't even been diagnosed yet. Studies have shown a connection between using those drugs and cardiovascular disease. It can also cause death. I can't just sit idly by and let her give it to him... and she can't hear me even though I've shouted this to her at the top of my lungs. The only thing I can do is hide the darn stuff so she can't find it."

"OK, I think I understand... you are here to protect Jerry," Becky acknowledged.

"Protect him from what?" Paulie sobbed.

"From you, you dumb blonde," Mary Beth shot back. When she looked back at Becky, she smiled and said, "I guess I've been a little jealous since Jerry remarried. I've had to suck it up and would've kept quiet until this crazy new wife gave him something that could kill him."

"Come on now," Becky appeased, "let's not be nasty. Paulie loves Jerry and would never do anything to harm him. Right, Paulie."

"I would never hurt Jerry. I love him with all my heart," she vowed.

"Mary Beth has some input into Jerry's condition," Becky acknowledged and then repeated the late wife's assessment to Paulie.

"Oh my goodness!" Paulie exclaimed. "Then she was trying to stop me from giving him something that would hurt him … even kill him?"

"Exactly," Mary Beth replied.

"That's it in a nutshell," Becky agreed.

"It's not good for him to sleep so much," Mary Beth added. "He gets like that on occasion. She should wake him up, get him moving. His depression only gets worse if he's left on his own so much. She can't baby him."

Becky turned to Paulie, "Can you wake him up?"

"Sure, but is that the best thing to do?" Paulie asked.

"Mary Beth thinks that it is. You must remember that she was married to him for many years. She might have some good counsel and guidance to offer," Becky advised.

Paulie gently shook Jerry by the shoulder, "Jerry, honey, can you wake up?"

He roused and looked around the room at Mary Beth, Paulie, Jennifer, and Becky. "Am I dying or already dead?" he asked. "Is that Mary Beth too? Have you come to take me home, Bethy?"

"No, you lazy bum. Quit worrying these people to death and get up and keep on living!" Mary Beth hotly replied. "You have a lot to be grateful for and a good many years to live if you'll take care of yourself. Now, stop this idiocy and get on with it. Tell Paulie to force him to get up and do things. She has to keep him moving. He gets lazy and obstinate, but if she wants him to last, she has to ride him hard." With those final words, Mary Beth cackled and was gone.

Meanwhile, back at Bobby's, Patrick asked, "What's this all about, Bobby?"

"Oh, just a little experiment," Bobby replied. He was in a jovial mood and couldn't wait to see if his theory was accurate. "Come on in. I need you to see something. Well actually, I need you to feel something. He laughed and patted Patrick on the back.

Chapter 35

While Becky had been at work on Monday, Barbara was in Asheville that day as well. She'd come home early to help Becky with the Christmas dinner. Well, in reality, she wouldn't cook or bake a thing, but she could help out by shopping and gathering the ingredients Becky needed to prepare their meal.

As Barb rushed around town to grocery shop, she also felt hopelessly cheerful. She was surprised at those feelings after everything that had happened with Marty.

She'd expected to be in the doldrums, a depressed, sluggish state for ages. However, when the mood lifted, it had risen so high that the weight was completely gone. She felt alive.

After she'd unloaded the groceries and put them away, Barb decided that the Christmas meal called for a little something extra special. She really wanted to make it up to Becky after she'd spoiled her Thanksgiving dinner. With that in mind, she headed out to the Asheville Wine Market located on Biltmore Avenue.

While Barb perused sections arranged by region, she wondered how she'd choose the perfect wine from the row-after-row of quality hand-picked vinos. According to the advertisement, the owners made their selections from independent, often family-run vignerons. Engrossed in the selection process, she didn't notice that she was being stalked until a calm deep voice asked, "Making a selection for your family Christmas dinner?"

"So much to choose from," Barb sighed before she looked up and into warm hazel eyes that seemed to twinkle from the reflection of the strung holiday lighting.

"Maybe I can help," he offered. Then added, "Hello and Merry Christmas. I'm Christopher."

"Merry Christmas, Christopher. I'm Barbara Tibbs."

"What's the main course?" he asked.

"Wait, do you work here?"

He laughed cheerfully before replying, "Not at all, but I do know a bit about wines. Perhaps I can help you select the best option for your particular situation."

"Well, that would be lovely because I'm at a loss. Our Thanksgiving dinner was a disaster and I'd like this one to be special," she paused to wonder why she was telling him this, but it felt good to confess her sins to a stranger. "I'd like to make it up to my younger sister. You see, she's vegetarian and even though she prepared the last family meal, I spoiled it for her by bringing meat to the table."

"I take it that this is a recent lifestyle change," he acknowledged.

"Very perceptive," Barb silently noticed as she nodded her response.

"Then, I suggest a nice red wine. Maybe a Merlot or Gamay. Now, if you plan to surprise her with a turkey or goose added to her table, then I'd suggest a red Burgundy."

"I'm not going to surprise her again," Barb sighed. "I think I learned my lesson last time."

"Did it really cause that much upset?" his warm eyes wanted to know. Strangely enough, she felt like telling him.

"It's a long story."

"And, I bet I'd love to hear it. Let's pick out some wine and then grab a coffee in the back. There's a barista back there and some seating. As chilly as the weather has turned since sunset, I could use a hot cup. How about you?"

"I think I'd like that."

Christopher helped her with the selections and then they went to the back as he'd suggested. After he'd ordered them each a Caffe breve, espresso with steamed half-and-half, he returned to the table.

"Oh, that's delicious," Barb exhaled.

"That's the way I like it too. Now, unburden yourself. Tell me about the Thanksgiving fiasco."

"Well, in order to get the full importance, you'd have to know our history," she began. "You see, I'm the oldest of the Tibbs children. I have a brother named Bobby who is two years younger and a sister named Becky who is four years younger. It all started the night our parents died in a traffic accident six years ago...," and she did unburden herself. She told this man, a complete stranger, everything that she'd wanted to tell Marty but couldn't.

As Barbara confessed her deepest family secrets, Christopher listened more intently than he'd ever listened to anyone. The events this beautiful woman sitting across from him shared were shocking and revealing. He felt as if he'd been given a personal message from the universe. He'd had so many questions, so much worry, that he felt relieved as well. He stared into her startling blue eyes and got lost for a while.

When Barbara had finished the tale, he said, "I must meet the rest of your family. I would love to meet Bobby and Becky."

"You're serious," Barb stated.

"I am. I've never been more serious in my life."

"I don't understand why that would be important to you," she admitted. "I mean, we just met in a wine store and had coffee together, but I don't think that qualifies as a prelude to meeting the family." She chuckled at her own boldness.

"You've just admitted that you've told me more in thirty minutes than you ever told your lifelong sweetheart the entire time you knew him. I think that quantifies as a prelude."

"Yes, but I'm not sure how Bobby and Becky will see it. They might not want a complete stranger knowing their business and secrets."

"Do you really consider me a stranger after all we've shared?" Christopher asked as he held her gaze.

"You know everything about me, but I don't know anything about you," she countered.

"I recently moved to the area to take a teaching position at UNC. I'm thirty-four years old. My family is from New England. I'm an only child and grandson. I love good coffee and fine wine. And more importantly, you've struck a chord in my soul. You see, Barbara, I lost someone very special to me too. Only my loss was from her death. I needed to know that the things you told me were real. I believe that Anne is still here and I'm at a loss as to how I can help her find peace and move on."

As he spoke, a young woman appeared behind him. Barbara clearly saw her. She was in her thirties with long, blonde hair and a pretty oval face. She gently stroked his hair and he unconsciously waved the spidery feeling away. The ghost giggled and continued to stroke his hair.

Barbara took a deep breath as she remembered the things Becky had said only a few days ago, "Help one ghost, just one." She hadn't had time to wrap her head around it yet, but she couldn't deny the opportunity right in front of her. After the detailed constructive criticism from her siblings, she'd made a concerted effort to moderate the amount of medication she took. If she wanted to see ghosts, decreasing her dosage had worked.

"If Anne has long, blonde hair and a pretty face, she is here," Barb advised.

"You can see her?"

"Yes, she is standing behind you and stroking your hair. That spider web feeling you get is her petting you."

"I thought that was one of the signs she was still around, but I wasn't certain."

"I try not to talk when I'm around him," Anne whispered. "I think it hurts his ears and I don't know how to moderate it."

They were talking at the same time.

"There are lots of ghost rules, Anne, but I'm not the one who is best equipped to explain anything. That would be my younger sister Becky," Barb admitted. "But I can tell both of you that when you talk at the same time, it's more difficult for me to hear either of you." She smiled to soften the reproach.

"I promise to remain silent unless you ask me a direct question," Christopher apologized.

"Oh, don't worry. I'm just excited that someone can finally see me," Anne exclaimed. And, as her voice rang out, Christopher grabbed his ears as if in pain. "See?" she expressed her regret, "my voice hurts him."

Barbara didn't know the solution for sure, but she assumed that it was Anne's eagerness that caused a certain frequency that was painful to Christopher. She told Anne her supposition and added, "Perhaps if you tone down your enthusiasm, it will help."

"I think I understand," Anne said in a calm, natural voice. "Like that?"

"That seemed to work. Now, is there anything you wish Christopher to know? Do you have any unfinished business with him?"

"I want him to move on. I want him to love again and find happiness. He's too young to grieve over me. I don't think I can leave him until I know that he'll be all right."

"How long has it been?" Barb asked.

"Goodness, I don't know. It's different here. There really isn't a way to tell time."

"Christopher, how long has it been since Anne's death?"

"Three years," he answered. "Three long years."

"I can't stand to see him so sad!" Anne once again let her emotions affect her voice. Christopher grabbed his ears again.

"Why does that happen?" he exclaimed.

"Anne is very excited. When her voice is overly enthusiastic, the frequency hurts your ears. She is aware and she'd trying to moderate her reactions."

"Is she sad, angry, or confused?" His voice was tormented with worry.

"No, she just admitted that she wants you to move on, to find happiness with someone else." Barb directed her questions back to Anne, "Christopher says that you died three years ago. Your worry for him has kept you here. Do you think that you can let him go? Can you move on to a better life the same as you wish for him?"

Anne was confused. "I am in a better life. Here there isn't any pain or nausea from the chemo. I sleep a lot and nothing bothers me … until I remember Christopher. Then I have to find him and make sure he is all right."

"That's my point, Anne. You're not letting him go so he can let you go. Each time you come to him, even though he can't see you, he feels you. He remembers you and what you meant to him. Those old feelings of love are rekindled and he misses you all over again. He grieves all over again. If you truly want him to be happy, then you must let him go."

"I don't intend to do that," Anne sorrowfully admitted. "I didn't' know that I was doing it. I'm so sorry. How do I let him go? How do I move to that better place that you mentioned?"

"Have you seen any doorways?" Barb asked.

"Yes, but I was afraid so I didn't check them out."

"The next time you see a doorway, look into it. You should see someone you know on the other side of it. They are waiting for you. Go to them and that is the true peace you will find. That is how you let Christopher go."

Barbara wasn't sure where the words came from or how she knew the things she knew, but she went with it and allowed the experience to flow out of her.

"My goodness," Anne choked, "as soon as you said that a doorway appeared. What do I do now?"

"Do you see anyone you know?"

"I see my grandmother and grandfather," Anne replied.

"You are free to go to them, Anne."

As she spoke the words, Anne moved away and disappeared.

"She's gone, Christopher. Anne has crossed over and she's really gone. You will both find peace now. And, speaking of being gone, I have to go also. It's almost eight o'clock and Becky will be home. It was nice to meet you."

Barbara stood and hurried away leaving Christopher seated and speechless. She didn't even give him the chance or opportunity to say thanks.

Chapter 36

Christmas day, Barbara, Bobby Hillary, and Rings had already arrived at Becky's for dinner before Patrick got there. Bobby had built a roaring fire and he sat with Hillary on the hearth while Barbara opened a bottle of wine. At times, the heat was too much and Bobby stood and moved away to cool off his backside. Hillary did the same and they giggled like kids who couldn't resist returning to the source of fun. When the doorbell rang, Becky eagerly rushed to answer it.

Patrick stood on the stoop holding a medium-sized white box with a bright pink ribbon tied around it. Becky gasped and then apologized, "Oh, I'm so sorry, I didn't even think to get you anything. I'm a terrible girlfriend."

"At least you're my girlfriend," he smiled a dimpled grin.

"Come in out of the cold," she urged.

As he entered the warm family room he explained, "Becky, I hope you like this present. It's sort of a combined gift from me and Bobby. I'm sure he'll tell you all about it during dinner. I need you to open it right away, so if you don't like it you can blame him and if you love it, you'll kiss me for the small part I played in procuring it."

"All right," she replied as she reached to take the box from Patrick.

"No," he encouraged, "you need to be seated before you open it."

Becky went to the sofa and sat down, and then she patted the spot next to her and encouraged him to sit with her. "I'm ready."

Patrick sat the box in her lap and smiled again, "I really do hope you like it."

"You're scaring me," she admitted as she untied the bow and opened a corner of the box. She couldn't believe her eyes when she spied the cute white kitten curled up asleep on a pink blanket that matched her nose and ears.

"I wish I could see her," Patrick admitted, "but you can and that's what counts."

"She's beautiful," Becky sighed. "Where on earth did you find her?"

"During my first ghost case," Bobby answered.

"Why hasn't she crossed over?" Becky worried.

Hills had been chatting with Barb and neither of them heard most of the exchange between the other three.

Feeling left out, Hills demanded, "What is it?"

"A beautiful kitten," Becky breathed. "She's all white, fluffy fur with pink tipped ears and nose. A little girl. How adorable!"

"There are no holes in the box. Are you nuts?" Hills exclaimed. "Is she still alive? You should've put some air holes, you big dummy!"

"She's fine," Bobby shushed Hillary. "She's just sleeping."

"What's her name?"

"Prissy," Bobby and Patrick replied in unison.

"Can I touch her?" Hills asked moving closer.

"You have to touch everything," Bobby teased. "Like a kid, putting your fingers everywhere."

"TMI," Barb laughed.

Hillary nudged Bobby aside and came closer to look into the box, "I can't see anything except a pink blanket. Wait, you found a ghost kitty?" Hills asked in surprise, "and you didn't even tell me about it?"

"See, we didn't need any air holes," Patrick said.

"It was a surprise," Bobby defended as Hills poked him on the shoulder.

"I get it," she said. "But keep in mind that I don't like secrets."

"I get it," he replied and then added, "I'll tell y'all all about it over dinner. Let's eat, I'm starving!"

They gathered at the dining table and Barbara and Hills helped Becky serve the dishes. Bobby carved the turkey and Patrick carved the ham that he'd brought earlier so it would have time to warm in the oven. As soon as everything was ready, the Tibbs' ancestors appeared; they filled the room with good wishes for a Merry Christmas and a prosperous New Year.

"Our family is here to wish us good tidings," Becky added for Patrick and Hillary's benefit. "My father, Justin Tibbs, is saying grace," she whispered and everyone bowed their heads. Then Becky blessed all the ancestors with love and light as Zetmeh had stressed the importance of it. When that was complete the ancestors quickly departed, including their parents, Justin and Joyce.

Becky silently counted her blessings. She'd never been happier and that joy welled up inside her as tears spilled down her face.

"What's wrong?" Patrick asked.

"Nothing," Becky replied, "absolutely nothing."

Just as Bobby had promised to do, he shared the adventures of his first ghost case with everyone while they ate the lovely dishes Becky had prepared. In conclusion, he added, "I knew if Prissy bonded with Patrick then she was the kitten for you, Becky. I had him come over Monday night to check out my theory. And, the little princess fell in love with him."

"I fell for her too," Patrick admitted. "She's sweet and adorable just like her new owner. It's a perfect match."

"How did you know that, Bobby?" Becky asked.

"I can't explain it. I just knew she was meant for you even though she jumped into my arms rather than cross over with Sue Ellen. I really can't explain it any better than that," Bobby claimed.

Zetmeh advised:

> *Your brother is unaware of all the changes that have taken place, dear one. However, just as you became more open to the spiritual world, he has done the same. He is now encouraged and guided more closely by his own spirit guides. This is a wondrous event in his growth, both spiritual and personal.*

Then, to everyone's surprise, Barbara had her own ghost story to tell. They listened closely as she described her encounter with Christopher.

When the tale was finished, Becky looked at Barb accusingly and gasped, "Did you find him attractive? Did you get his name and number? Did you give him a chance to ask for yours! I swear, Barbara! You probably missed a perfect opportunity to meet someone new."

"No," Bobby added. "I can tell you she didn't. She just walked out of the wine market without looking back."

"You know me too well, brother," Barb sighed.

After their stories were finished, both looked at Becky with even more respect for the job she'd done. Then, Barbara said, "There is so much I don't know about this work. You'll give us some tips if we decide to keep helping ghosts?"

"I know I could use some too," Bobby agreed.

"Does this mean that you will help other ghosts?" Becky asked.

"I can't make any promises, but I did not find helping Christopher repulsive or distasteful."

"Neither did I," Bobby agreed. "I enjoyed helping Sue Ellen and Prissy. I didn't know how to bring down the light, but fortunately for Sue Ellen, her family came to greet her."

"Wait, Hillary asked, "Do you mean that you have to open a doorway for all ghosts or they get stuck here?"

"No," Becky answered. "Most people don't need that help. They just cross over or their family meets them. It depends on their beliefs. If they believe they are going to a better place, they do. If they believe that when they die they are just dead, then their spirit doesn't know what to do next so they linger. Those are the ghosts we usually help. Some are left behind because their deaths were shocking and they didn't know they were going to die. As for you two," she said as she looked at Bobby and Barb, "you know I will help in any way I can," Becky promised as she got up to serve dessert and coffee.

"Oh, my goodness, Becky!" Barb exclaimed. "This brings back so many memories. It tastes exactly like I remember grandmother's date nut candy!"

"Where'd you get the recipe?" Bobby asked.

"Grandmother Tibbs generously shared it with me," Becky grinned.

Bobby cackled before he said, 'Remember how she used to come into the kitchen with a wooden spoon?"

"Are you kids in that candy again? You know it's for the adults in the family!" Barb, Bobby, and Becky screeched at the same time as they mimicked their favorite grandmother.

"She hit me once with that spoon," Bobby added.

"No!" Becky protested.

"That's because you were tough and hardheaded even as a child," Barb giggled. "She had to do something to get through to you." They all laughed again.

"Well, heck," Hills chuckled, "that's certainly one way to keep the family secrets in the family. When my grandparents died, we lost so much, including all their old-time recipes and stories."

"Yeah, it's hard to hold onto those," Bobby sympathized.

"You guys certainly have the advantage," Hills wistfully acknowledged. "Do you suppose that I could talk to my grandmother through one of you?"

Bobby thoughtfully nodded as he patted her hand.

"It's delicious," Patrick added to ease the tension and melancholy that had suddenly descended on them. "What's in it, or rather, how do you make it? I've never had anything like this."

"It's really simple," Becky advised. "Let's see, there's two cups sugar, either brown or white, a cup of whole organic milk, and a quarter cup of real butter. Boil that to a soft-ball stage which usually takes about twenty to thirty minutes. Remove from heat and add one cup chopped, pitted dates, one cup chopped pecans or walnuts, and one teaspoon of vanilla extract. Stir that in and spread the mixture out on a clean, damp section of cheesecloth. I didn't have any so I used parchment paper dusted with confectioner's sugar. It starts to cool almost immediately, so you roll it into a tight log and refrigerate for at least eight hours or overnight. Once it's solid, slice it into thick rounds like this. That's really all there is to it."

"Yum," everyone moaned as they took another bite. "I'm so happy that you like it."

After dinner, they went to the patio to drink hot cocoa and celebrate their latest tradition with the twinkle lights shining love on each one of them. Patrick wrapped strong arms around Becky to help keep her warm and Hills snuggled closer to Bobby. Barbara was happy for both of the couples and didn't envy their newfound relationships.

For the first time since their parents' death, she felt hopeful that she'd find her own real love too.

"Look at them," she whispered, as she indicated Rings and Prissy through the window. They'd previously been playfully chasing each other around the fireplace, nipping, scratching, and biting each other, but now the pair lay curled up together before the hearth. Prissy was between the pup's large feet and his head rested across her neck. "Isn't that precious?"

###

Thank you for reading this book. If you enjoyed Becky's story, please leave a review. Reviews are vrey important to every author. I know they are to me. It lets me know that you want me to continue the story.

You can read more about this North Carolina medium on the series page listed on Amazon. Or visit my website at chariss.com to subscribe to my newsletter. I send out a small newsletter once or twice a month telling you about my new releases and the books that I have on sale that month.

Keep reading for a sneak peek at The Journey.

Chariss K. Walker

A Sneak Peek at *The Journey*

Chapter 1

Katherine Rutherford Barrett thought life was good. She was happy with the life she had made for herself and her daughter, Samantha. She was not looking for anything else, but she had unexpectedly found love again. Love was something she'd thought lost to her forever. She had no idea what a rude and harsh awakening was ahead. When it hit, the reality blindsided her.

Affectionately called Katy by her family, she'd lost a lot over the last eleven years. Her husband, Hank Barrett, died while on active duty in the military. She was pregnant at the time of his death and Hank never met his daughter. Hank and Katy knew they were having a baby girl and they both agreed to name her Samantha and nickname her 'Sammy' to honor his older brother who died while serving his country.

She had to go through years of red tape to finally succeed in obtaining Hank's military benefits, his life insurance payout, and Dependency and Indemnity Compensation (DIC). In the meantime, she'd relied on her parents for help and support.

Hank didn't have any relatives that could help Katy. His father left when he was ten and Sammy was sixteen. They didn't know whether he was dead or alive. Their mother, worn-out and exhausted from the struggles of a single mother, had died only eight years later. Without resources and other options, Sammy encouraged Hank to enlist. Three years later, Sammy was killed in action while serving in the Gulf War.

Hank had already served eight years when he and Katy met. He was still enlisted, but being stateside, he took advantage of the veteran educational benefit and arranged college classes around his military schedule. They met during her second year at Jacksonville University.

Hank, polite, disciplined, and handsome, was exactly what Katy needed at the time. She was looking for something more than the rebellious years recently experienced. She'd gone a little wild during the first few years away from home and without parental supervision.

They dated until both graduated in their perspective fields. With diplomas in hand, the couple quickly married in Ft. Pierce, Florida. Katy's parents, Josh and Susan Rutherford looked on with approval. They knew Hank would take good care of their only child. He was mature and had a good career in the military. They had no way of knowing that Hank would not return from that tour in Afghanistan,

Katy was devastated by her husband's death, but reality closely followed on its heels – The reality that she had no idea what to do. She was alone with a newborn baby and had very little money. How would she make ends meet? So far, she had been unable to collect on Hank's military benefits. When Josh and Susan saw the dilemma their daughter faced, they willingly gave the assistance needed. Katy was truly grateful for that... and the many other ways her parents filled the loss of her husband.

Often, parents are reluctant to allow their grown children to return home again but this case was different. Josh and Susan invited Katy, and their newborn granddaughter, Sammy, to live in the cottage situated directly behind the family home. It was usually reserved for in-laws' visits, but times were desperate for Katy and Sammy. The Rutherford's freely opened their home, hearts, and lives to the small family.

Josh and Susan offered to babysit Sammy while Katy worked as a bookkeeper for one of the large citrus groves in Ft. Pierce. They also offered to babysit so that Katy could have a bit of social life. She was very thin and pale. The only time she smiled or laughed was when she looked adoringly at her baby girl. Although grateful that her parents kept Sammy while she worked, Katy was too tired after the long days and simply wanted to be home with her only child after work was done. And, when she did have a social life, Katy preferred that Sammy and her parents were included.

Susan prepared the evening meals and Katy dined with them. Occasionally, on Friday nights, the family dined at one of the local restaurants along the Indian River. The cottage where Katy and Sammy lived had only a small kitchenette and wasn't equipped for more than making coffee and toasting bread. It was outfitted with a small dinette set and a separate bedroom to the right with a screened-in porch. The bathroom was on the opposite end of the cottage near the kitchen. Josh had built the cottage and plumbed it for convenience, not practicality. For the last several years, it was home to Katy and Sammy.

After the long wait to get Hank's much-deserved benefits, Katy offered to buy a home of her own and move out, but Josh and Susan were now settled into this new life. They didn't want Katy and Sammy to leave. They enjoyed the responsibility of watching over their granddaughter and couldn't imagine how their retirement would feel without her in their lives. Sammy gave new purpose to her grandparents.

Days once spent fishing or working in the garden, were now spent making sure Sammy had a good breakfast and did her homework before Katy got home from work. Since Katy left for work at seven each morning, either Josh or Susan drove Sammy to school and picked her up each afternoon. With a new rhythm to their lives, they felt needed and wanted for the first time since Katy left for college. They reassured her that she and Sammy were welcome to stay as long as they liked.

Rather than buy a new home, Katy listened to her father's investment advice. She had the DIC monthly stipend direct-deposited into an investment account as he suggested. It became a 'rainy day' fund. Without rental expenses, utilities, and very little food costs, Katy and Sammy easily lived on her paycheck from the citrus grove. It was a good living. They had all that they needed, except for the love of a husband and father.

Chapter 2

Eight years into the arrangement, tragedy struck. Josh and Susan went to Ft. Lauderdale to get supplies. Katy had a 'bad feeling' about the trip and asked them not to go that day, but they'd given her a warm hug and told her not to worry.

While still at work, Katy got a call from the school. No one came to pick up Sammy that afternoon. She rushed to her daughter's school. She tried her parents' cell phones repeatedly but didn't get an answer. Later that evening, while she and Sammy paced her parents' home, a highway patrol car pulled up. The 'bad feeling' was now a reality. Josh and Susan were involved in a four-car pile-up on Interstate-95 South. Both were killed instantly.

She listened to the notification news and wiped away tears. She confirmed that she'd go to the morgue for the identification process. Then she held her daughter close as they cried together over the great loss that had come too soon. She couldn't believe it, and yet, she knew it was true. Why didn't her parents listen to her when she'd tried to warn them?

Later, when Katy looked through the paperwork in Josh's desk, she found everything she needed in a large folder, including their wills and final instructions for burial. Josh and Susan had gone several years earlier to make their final arrangements and update their wills to include Sammy in the estate. Katy was grateful for that, but she couldn't stop crying.

Living at home again with her parents had forged a strong bond of love. When only a sullen teenager, they'd never had that same connection. Then, she couldn't wait to leave home, to head off to college, and get away from them. Now, she missed them terribly and so did Sammy. During the last eight years, they'd become surrogate parents to their grandchild. Katy realized she was crying for her own loss, but she couldn't help it.

After the funeral, Katy and Sammy met with the family attorney, James Kegel, and listened closely as he explained Josh and Susan's wishes. The estate left for Sammy would remain in trust until she was twenty-one years old. Before that age, the funds could only be used to pay for college tuition. The home was left to Katy. If she decided to sell it, half the proceeds from the sale would go into an already established trust for Sammy.

When it was all said and done, Josh and Susan had left a moderate estate and neither their daughter nor granddaughter would ever be without the things they needed again. Their final wishes had been a blessing to that end. Still, Katy couldn't think about that right now. Their deaths were too fresh in her mind. However, she did have to consider the family home. At Sammy's insistence, they moved into it the following weekend.

"It's what Grandpa and Grandma would want," Sammy said with conviction and Katy realized that her daughter was right. For an eight-year-old child, Sammy was incredibly mature. It was only to be expected since she'd been surrounded by adults most of her life.

Sammy was a beautiful child with perfect features. Her dark hair was thick and shiny, hanging down her back to the waist. She had a creamy complexion and a heart-shaped face with thick lashes that framed clear green eyes, like her mother. And yet, Sammy had a definite 'tom-boy' thing going on.

She preferred jeans and a tee-shirt, refusing to wear dresses from the time she was two years old. She'd followed her Grandpa Josh around after school and on weekends and even had a certain swagger that was similar to his walk. Katy found these traits endearing and adorable. There wasn't anything at all that she'd change about Sammy.

After the death of her parents, the home reminded Katy of them every day, but it wasn't a bad reminder. It was comforting. She could still feel their love and care all around her. Sammy took Katy's childhood room and Katy took her parents' master bedroom. She refurbished and updated the rooms with new beds and dressing, but left most of the home the way it was. Susan was a natural decorator and everything was in pristine condition anyway. It didn't need much improvement.

Katy began to work fewer hours at the citrus grove so that she could take Sammy to and from school each day. The first year went by quickly and Sammy transitioned from third to fourth grade with ease. During that first summer, they took a short vacation to the Florida Keys and stayed at the Silver Palms Hotel. The hotel was within walking distance to all the colorful city had to offer.

Katy and Sammy walked hand in hand, taking in the sights. They visited Hemmingway's home and observed the Southernmost Point Marker. The large concrete buoy was the closest spot in the US to Cuba, which was only ninety miles away. They rode bikes and swam in the nearly deserted, huge hotel pool. It was a time to relax and refresh. It was a time to heal after everything that had happened that year. Especially after the deaths of Josh and Susan.

This vacation became a ritual for the next several summers, and soon, Sammy's fifth grade was nearing an end. With only a few more months before summer vacation, Katy felt a little overwhelmed that Sammy would soon enter her first year of middle school.

Middle School!

It was a vast structure where all the elementary schools in the area converged into one massive group of sixth, seventh, and eighth-graders. It would be a huge transition for any child and Katy worried about how her daughter would manage the new school environment. She also wondered how she would handle this newest transition in Sammy's life.

Chapter 3

During March, the weather grew warm and sunny. Katy and Sammy continued with Josh and Susan's tradition by dining out on Friday afternoons at one of the many Indian River restaurants they'd frequented together as a family. They often sat on the open-air decks to soak up the afternoon sun. To anyone observing them, it was apparent the mother and daughter were content with the life they shared.

Katy was very youthful—she could've been mistaken as an older sister to Sammy. They had the same clear green eyes and dark, shiny hair framing heart-shaped. It was during one of those dining-out experiences that Katy caught the eye of Chuck Reeves.

Chuck was tall and handsome with dark brown hair and hazel eyes. His face was often a mask of pleasantry as he kept his emotions and thoughts closely guarded. He watched the mother-daughter exchanges silently and on the sly. He didn't make his presence known then but instead inquired about the two girls who obviously had a strong familial bond. That was the first of several times he watched them from afar. One Friday evening, after Katy and Sammy finished their evening meal, Chuck had a drinking buddy drive him as they followed the young mother and her daughter home.

"Don't get paranoid," he jokingly told the friend. "I only want to see where they live."

A few weeks later, Chuck sat in a more open area and sent a note to their table as soon as Katy and Sammy were seated. The note asked for an introduction even though his previous inquiries had already garnered their names. He already knew the mother was Katy and the daughter was Sammy. He also knew where they lived and that Katy's parents had been killed in a terrible crash on Interstate-95. He knew that Katy's husband died before their daughter was born. Chuck knew a great deal of other trivia also. After all, it was a small town and people liked to talk about the tragedies of others easily enough when you bought them a drink.

"What's your name?" Katy read the slip of paper before refolding it. She surreptitiously looked around the open-aired deck. An eager, smiling face was only a few tables away. Chuck raised his hand in greeting and nodded. She reflexively smiled, but quickly looked away. She dropped the note on a serving tray without answering it.

The next time they dined out, Chuck tried a different approach. He sent a note with his name and a little information about himself: *I'm Chuck Reeves. I'm thirty-six years old. I'm a supervisor in the construction industry. I'm originally from Asheville, North Carolina.*

Katy read the note, but still, she didn't respond. She wasn't sure she wanted anything else in her life right then. She and Sammy were content and satisfied with things the way they were. She had a good job. They were happy. Even with the prospect of middle school hanging over both their heads, they liked their established routine. Katy sometimes wondered if she was more nervous and concerned about the changes on the horizon than Sammy was.

She didn't long for love or a relationship the way some of her friends at work did. She was comfortable with her life. She wasn't out looking for more. She didn't hope that a man would somehow fill a void. There wasn't a void to fill. Things were good the way they were.

As they dined, Katy glanced at Chuck on a few occasions, but she didn't see any potential there. Although he dressed neatly in jeans and spotless work boots, a polo-style shirt, and was handsome, she easily dismissed him and his insistency. She wasn't interested in a relationship.

That would change.

Chuck made sure of it. Over the next few weeks, it didn't matter which restaurant Katy and Sammy chose; they always ran into this very determined man. Still unwilling to give up, Chuck sent the note to Sammy, asking her to intercede on his behalf. He was very persistent; Katy had to give him that. She took the note from Sammy and finally responded with her name and age. That was all the encouragement it took, and although Chuck only nodded when he read the message, he knew he'd won a great victory. He'd cracked Katy's protective shell.

The next weekend, he was prepared. He brought a bouquet of flowers to their table in person. It had been a long time since she'd received flowers. Something about the gesture melted a small spot in Katy's heart. Against her better judgment, she finally relented. From then on, Chuck Reeves became a member of their party each time he chanced to be at the same restaurant, which was often.

Now, he didn't wait for an invitation, he simply joined them as soon as they were seated. Katy wondered how he knew where they dined each Friday. Admittedly, it was a small town and the information was easy to discover.

Chuck inched closer and closer. Soon, he paid for their meals. Next, he planned where and when they dined. Reluctant in the beginning, Katy felt flattered by the lavish and thoughtful attention. His romantic interest eroded her resistance.

Sammy, now eleven years old, reserved her opinion about Chuck Reeves, but she was cordial to the new person who seemed intent on gaining her mother's affection. It was a new experience for Sammy because she didn't recall ever seeing her mother with any man other than Grandpa. Katy had certainly never dated anyone. Although she'd seen many pictures of him in photo albums, Sammy didn't remember her father at all. When asked, her grandparents agreed he was 'a very nice man.' Sammy had learned not to judge 'newness' right away; she'd 'wait-and-see,' as her Grandma would've said.

By late-April, Chuck took them to dinner in his dark-blue king cab pickup. He was courteous, energetic, and always offered to lend a hand. Even though Katy and Sammy preferred to dine along the river, they went along with his idea of a better restaurant when he took them to nice restaurants along the beach.

Everywhere they went the locals greeted him by name. The other patrons were friendly to Chuck, and therefore, courteous to Katy and Sammy by association. After so many dark days, Katy liked the attention. Seeing so many people who seemed to know, like, and respect Chuck mistakenly had confirmed he was worth knowing. Katy misread the entire situation…Even though popular on the surface, generally, Chuck wasn't well-liked.

This concludes the excerpt.

If you enjoyed The Journey, you can find the completed book on Amazon.

About the Author

2018 B.R.A.G. Medallion Honoree

Award-winning author, Chariss K. Walker, M.Msc., Reiki Master/Teacher writes both fiction and nonfiction books with a metaphysical and spiritual component. Her fiction expresses a visionary/metaphysical message that illustrates the growth in a character's consciousness while utilizing a paranormal aspect. Her nonfiction books share insight, hope, and inspiration. Even though Chariss writes dark-fiction about insanely dark topics, such as sexual abuse, incest, pedophilia, sexual assault, and other inappropriate dinner conversation, there is always an essential question of the abstract nature that gives a reader increasing awareness and perception. All of her books are sold worldwide in eBook, paperback, and many are in large print.

You can learn more about Chariss at her website: www.chariss.com

You can find Chariss K. Walker at the following social media site:

Facebook
Goodreads
BookBub
Twitter
Instagram

Other books by Chariss K. Walker

Fiction Books:

The Vision Chronicles – Paranormal Metaphysical Thrillers
Kaleidoscope, Book 1
Spyglass, Book 2
Window's Pane, Book 3
Windows All Around, Book 4
Open Spaces, Book 5
Stream of Light, Book 6
Lamp's Light, Book 7
Clear Glass, Book 8

The Retreat
The Journey

Becky Tibbs: A North Carolina Medium's Mystery Series:
A Medium's Birthday Surprise, Book 1
A Medium's Thanksgiving Table, Book 2
A Medium's Christmas Gift, Book 3
A Medium's Valentine's Day Delight, Book 4
A Medium's Easter Epiphany, Book 5
A Medium's 4th of July, Book 6
A Medium's Engagement, Book 7
A Medium's Wedding Day, Book 8
And More!

Dark Fiction Books:

An Alec Winters Series – Dark Supernatural
Suspense/Urban Fantasy:
Prelude, Book 1
Crescent City, Book 2
Port City, Book 3
Harbor City, Book 4

Serena McKay Novels - Dystopian Crime Female P.I.
Thrillers
Purple Kitty, Book 1
Blue Cadillac, Book 2

A Serena McKay Spin-off series:
Salazar (2121, Book 1)
Sondra, (2121, Book 2)
Dinah (2121, Book 3)

my name is tookie

Nonfiction Books:

A Beginner's Guide to Visualization
Chakra Basics
The Spiritual Gifts
Abundance
Many Paths to Healing
Keep the Faith
Make a Joyful Noise
Make a Joyful Noise Study Guide
Finding Serenity 3-Book Boxed-Set
Going Deeper 6-Book Series:
A Beginner's Guide to Releasing Trapped Emotions, #1
Release Chakra Trapped Emotions, #2
Release Common Disease Trapped Emotions, #3
Release Hindrances to Success, #4
Release Body Systems Trapped Emotions, #5
Release Mental Blocks, #6
Letting go of Pain

Made in the USA
Columbia, SC
05 July 2025

60349187R00100